21 tattoos

A NOVEL

MONICA BROUSSARD

ACORN PUBLISHING

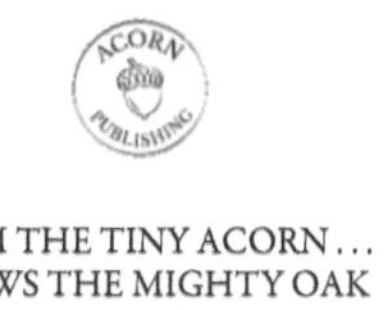

FROM THE TINY ACORN . . .
GROWS THE MIGHTY OAK

www.AcornPublishingLLC.com

For information, address:
Acorn Publishing, LLC
3943 Irvine Blvd. Ste. 218
Irvine, CA 92602

ISBN-13: 979-8-88528-062-4 (hardcover)
ISBN-13: 979-8-88528-061-7 (paperback)
Library of Congress Control Number: 2023905821

I would like to dedicate this book

to my husband and family.

You are my source of inspiration.

I am truly grateful for

all your support and love.

Chapter 1

Daylight seeped from the dreary, overcast sky. As night descended, black clouds drew a veil across the stars. At last, they parted, and the darkness gave birth to a full moon surrounded by a shimmering halo.

A beam of soft lunar light pierced the glass patio doors of the motel room, illuminating dingy walls. An old shaman woman squatted in the middle of the room, preparing herself for a ritual that had been practiced by her tribe for the past ten thousand years. It would transport her to another world, a spiritual realm where the spirits of both good and evil dwelt.

Sitting back on the heels of her bare feet, knees drawn tightly to her chest, she reached for a large tibia bone adorned with beads. The other hand delved into her skirt pocket for a small chicken bone she had salvaged from the motel dumpster the night before. Grinding it slowly in a tiny stone bowl, she began a soft chant.

Next, she pulled out a pouch filled with powder and emptied its herbal contents. Using the jagged edge of the sharp tibia bone, she made a small cut in her finger and waited patiently for the droplet of blood to splash onto the pile of powder. She placed the bone against her thin brown lips. A whistle quavered across the room. Alternating between rhythmic chanting and clicking of her beads, the old woman stood up and made a slow circle around the bowl. The ceremonial dance would redefine the spiritual properties of her body, mind, and soul.

As she passed the dresser, she grabbed a water bottle and took a sip, then spat the liquid into the powder. The tibia bone that had once connected flesh and sinew, and which contained the essence of physical life, was now used to stir the roux of her potion. Dipping her first two fingers into the concoction, she scooped up a dab of paste and smeared it along her tattooed forehead. It would disguise her face from the evil spirits.

Her finger proceeded down the bridge of her nose, sweeping to the outside perimeter, then down to the chin. She did this first to one side, then to the other. Dipping her fingers in the paste once again, she crossed her arms. Starting at her shoulders, she ran the tips of her two fingers down her arms, all the while continuing her chanting.

The shaman woman had been designated the keeper of sacred knowledge, accumulated over thousands of years. Her role was to restore harmony in the world by dispelling toxic, negative energy and restoring it with healthy, constructive energy to keep the balance between man and nature through ritual laws of wisdom that extended beyond time and space.

In this place, and at this time, the shaman's goal was to manifest the reunion of a particular man's soul back to his body.

Powerful forces gathered, swirling around her. At the moment she pierced the veil of earthly reality, it forged an electromagnetic field that surrounded the old woman's body. In an altered state of consciousness, she became unaware of the external world. Eyes closed, she entered a dark trance. Spirits collided. Lightning flashed, followed by a deep clap of thunder.

It shattered her trance. She collapsed to the floor. In the instant before her head struck the corner of the dresser, she saw the man's face that would save her granddaughter.

Chapter 2

Dr. Derek Hollinger stepped out the front door of his West Los Angeles penthouse into the stark, elegant hallway. He checked the time on his cell phone, stuffed it into his workout jacket, then entered the waiting private elevator and jabbed the button.

The elevator descended; seconds later, the doors opened to an oasis of private cabanas framing a swimming pool with a full moon shimmering in the water. A solitary swimmer stroked through the specks of reflected light floating across the surface.

Hollinger quietly passed two empty massage tables, heading for a set of double glass doors that threw his own reflection back—a tall, sandy-haired man with vivid blue eyes and serious, unsmiling features. He flipped the wall switch of the darkened chamber beyond. LED lights bloomed across an array of exercise machines. Walking to the first, he began his rigorous daily circuit. Then he returned to his penthouse, showered, and headed out on his Harley.

The weekend ride down the Santa Monica coastline rewarded him with a view of surfers dotting the seascape like seals as he rode past the barren beaches. He could smell the salt air filtering up through his helmet. The cool, damp mist saturated his jeans and felt soothing after his morning workout.

Hollinger needed to put the world behind him, just for a little while. It was the first anniversary of the passing of his mentor and adoptive father, Dr. Christopher Casey. He had battled grief and loneliness all morning, but he had an important event to attend that evening and needed to clear his head.

As a teenager, Hollinger had almost been beaten to death by a gang. Dr. Casey performed multiple reconstructive surgeries on him and they'd grown very close. In later years, Casey had taken the aspiring young medical student under his wing. Hollinger knew that his own career as a world-class plastic surgeon owed a huge debt to the kindly older physician.

Now, Hollinger enjoyed the good life. He owned an apartment in one of the most prestigious buildings in West Los Angeles. From his 6,000-square-foot penthouse on the thirty-eighth floor, he enjoyed an unobstructed view of the city. The expansive floor-to-ceiling windows exposed every angle of the sweeping metropolis, the mountain vistas, and the Pacific Ocean beyond. At night, it became a magical panorama of twinkling lights.

It was an apartment made for entertaining guests—something Hollinger rarely did. Polished hardwood floors with natural stone accents swept into an unused massive kitchen with stainless steel appliances and quartz countertops. A Jacuzzi on the outside balcony of the master bedroom was mainly for exhausted, solitary soaks after long hours of surgery. The wraparound terraces had almost no furniture.

The penthouse's location on the far west side of Los Angeles, near the beaches, was touted by the real estate agent as one of the best places to live in California. Downtown L.A., with its wonderful eateries, hip cafés, charming restaurants, and numerous social venues, invited Derek to step out on the town anytime he felt the urge.

That urge never came. His only ventures out were occasional short rides on his Harley Davidson. The first time he sat on his motorcycle, it was love at first sight; legs stretched out to the pegs and arms extended to the bars, the fit was just right. He savored the feeling of freedom it gave him while gliding along the highway.

To an outsider, his life might look lonely. But the doctor relished his luxurious apartment and expensive toys—earned by two decades of perseverance, dedication, and suffering.

The cathartic ride along the coast restored his faith as he returned home to prepare for the evening. After a few hours of careful grooming and prepping, he climbed into his Bentley and dropped the Plastic Surgeons' Association Award dinner invitation on the passenger seat.

Derek drove down his neighborhood's palm-lined street, rounded the first corner and braked. A group of teenagers hovered in the intersection he needed to cross. He stiffened as he watched them through his aviator sunglasses. He slowly rolled closer. They would pause every other step to roughhouse and shove each other.

Hands gripped the mahogany steering wheel as the thirty-nine-year-old plastic surgeon felt a stab of anxiety. While he sat in refined luxury, observing the outside world through the barrier of a windshield, this ragtag group crossing the road represented what he feared most: the city's out-of-control youth.

Derek had grown weary of the glorification of violence and drugs. It suddenly became apparent to him that the young men's outward appearance reflected their inner state of mind. Like a scene from *Lord of the Flies*.

The doctor quickly reached for the button to raise the windows. A split second later, the group was upon him. They yanked the Bentley door handles from both sides. A leering face pressed up against the rising glass of the driver's side window.

An adrenaline rush shot through Derek's body. He flashed back twenty-five years to a day when he was just fourteen and a group of heavily tattooed men with shaved heads had suddenly surrounded him. The memory of being punched, kicked, and beaten reactivated the shock and pain of the attack. He could hear the loud cracks of his bones breaking. The men's derisive laughter played like a background soundtrack in his head until the thud of a fist slamming down on the hood of his Bentley yanked him back to the present. The doctor floored the accelerator. The Bentley lurched forward, sending the teens jumping out of the way, arms and legs flailing.

Small beads of sweat formed on his upper lip as he glanced into the rearview mirror. The group was still stumbling around and shouting after the Bentley. Tires screeched as he turned the corner, knees vibrating. He tried to relax his leg and eased off the gas. Loosening his clammy grip on the wheel, he turned the AC vent for a blast of cool air. Derek circled the hotel city block a couple of times, allowing his pulse to slow, before pulling into the driveway of the New Century Hotel for the evening's event.

He dragged himself out from behind the wheel, still weak-kneed and shaking, one hand braced against the top of the car door.

The uniformed valet waited patiently while he straightened his tie and smoothed down the lapels of his Hugo Boss tuxedo jacket. A quick glance at the bright, serene full moon provided the doctor with a small flicker of self-composure.

Derek stepped onto the sidewalk and started for the hotel entrance. An old woman approached. Her mouth was moving, but he couldn't understand what she was saying. Devoid of emotion, he looked down into her strangely painted face just as an explosion of pain went off in his head. It felt like an ice pick being driven into his brain. A viselike grip tugged on his arm.

In a panic, Derek made a violent push-pull motion. The whipping force sent the old woman catapulting away. He tried to regain his composure. His eyes blurred from the searing pain. He took a deep breath to slowly regain his vision only to find the old woman lying on the ground. Astonished and embarrassed, he bent down to examine her for injuries. The blood rushed back to his head. The old woman quickly reached into her bag and pulled out a rattle. She started shaking it in his face and chanting. Startled, he backed away. *She must have a mental disorder.*

The uniformed doorman stood watching the scene, his eyes wide in amazement. Desperate to escape the bizarre encounter, Derek impulsively strode up to him.

"Please make sure the old woman is all right," he muttered, slipping a crisp hundred-dollar bill into the white-gloved hand.

The doorman nodded. "Yes, sir. Thank you!"

Derek couldn't believe his bad luck. The most prestigious award of the year was being handed out—to him!—and he was being plagued by unstable panhandlers.

Once inside the lavish lobby, he made a beeline for the men's room. After splashing water on his face and combing his hair, the doctor examined himself in the mirror. He needed to reflect composure and poise despite the unnerving events of the last hour. With a last tug on his tuxedo jacket, he turned to exit.

The muffled sound of voices reverberated through the polished marbled lobby. He found the award dinner venue sign posted next to the directory on the map.

Outside the monstrous banquet room, he approached a table staffed with people who were there to welcome the doctors and to hand out name badges. Derek struggled with trembling fingers to peel the plastic backing off his name tag and press it on his lapel. His anxiety rose while scanning the impressive ten-thousand-square-foot ballroom, filled with what seemed to be hundreds of tables and chairs, for his assigned seat. Shortness of breath gave way to light-headedness and mounting pressure in his chest. The doctor loosened his tie. He exercised every day and prided himself on being fit, but now he felt on the verge of a heart attack.

He sat down, trying to maintain an air of dignity. With a trembling hand, he took a sip of water to help swallow his nausea. The surrounding tables began to fill with guests. Their bright smiles and too-loud chatter only made him feel worse. A choking sensation propelled him up from the chair. As he stood to leave, he heard someone call his name. Soaked in sweat, Derek ignored the greeting. Lost in a dark chasm, he barely remembered driving home and parking his car.

A head popped up from behind the security desk to check who had entered the lobby.

"Good evening, Dr. Hollinger," the security guard called out.

The doctor waved a hand and hit the button for the penthouse on the thirty-eighth floor. The elevator's sudden acceleration forced him to grab the handrail. He rested his head between his arms and tried to breathe deeply. When the elevator door opened, he stumbled out into the vestibule to the threshold of a solitary door.

His key found its mark. With a weak push, the door opened. The Hugo Boss tuxedo jacket slipped from his hand and dropped in a heap on the floor. He struggled to peel off the sweat-drenched shirt, irritated and disappointed that he'd missed the award ceremony because of a flu. He made his way to the bathroom just in time to vomit. Dizzy and disoriented, he stumbled over to his California King and collapsed into a fitful nightmare.

Trapped in a gigantic web, the doctor struggled to free his lassoed hands and feet from the silky glue. He could feel the perfectly woven silk threads vibrate, creating ripples in every direction. Derek instinctively knew that these vibrational waves would signal the lurking predator.

Terrified, he struggled like an ill-fated fly. With limited eyesight, the Goliath spider navigated toward its prey through the vibrations felt in its eight legs. With cunning dexterity, the creature mounted his victim, wrapping the doctor in silk, turning him round and round as if toying with its food. Then the spider lunged. Fangs sank into the doctor's thigh, causing waves of excruciating pain. It dragged him to the center of the web to be fed upon at its leisure. The doctor lay there as if left for dead.

He tried unsuccessfully to wake from the nightmare. Derek's

heart jackhammered in his chest. He tossed and turned, consumed with confusion, pain, and fear. Each new nightmare filled him with mounting anxiety. The conviction that these were his last hours of life exposed a barren landscape of misery, fueling even more vivid dreams.

The dread caused by the premonition of a painful death gave way to a sense of hopelessness. Dark thoughts of vulnerability and despair echoed through his mind. Lost and alone, he struggled for sanity.

His eyes opened for a moment of lucidity. The soft light of the full moon illuminated his bedroom. He stared up at the ceiling, shivering and wracked with pain. Unable to move, he fell back into unconsciousness.

It was dark when he woke again. He'd lost all concept of time. Was it the same night? The next? Just the act of dragging himself off the mattress used up all his strength. When he reached the bathroom, he weakly twisted the faucet, splashed water on his face, and reached for the towel next to the sink. While wiping his swollen, bloodshot eyes, another wave of nausea hit. Yellow bile burned his throat. Derek knew at that moment that he was in serious trouble.

He opened the medicine cabinet to look for the Tamiflu, tossing items onto the floor before he found the right one. His hands shook so badly, he could hardly manage the child-proof cap. Pills tumbled into the sink. He finally shook a couple into his unsteady palm, washing them down with a drink from the faucet. He settled back into his bed, only to descend into another fitful sleep besieged by nightmares and fever-fueled hallucinations.

A little after midnight, he tried to prop himself up against the pillows. His vision was so blurred, he could barely see the twinkling lights coming through the window of his darkened bedroom. Willing himself to get up, he slowly felt his way around the bed to the bathroom. Fumbling to find the light switch, it took another full minute for his eyes to adjust. As he stood in front of the sink, a wave of nausea hit so hard it propelled him toward the tub, convulsing with dry heaves.

With both hands, he reached out to steady himself on the sink. Derek squeezed his eyes tight, wondering dully if he was even truly awake. Leaning into the mirror, he opened them . . . and let out a horrified wail.

He stumbled over to the full-length mirror behind the door. The man looking back was covered from head to toe with tattoos. A snake wrapped around one arm. A spider clutched his neck. There were more, many more. As he stared, open-mouthed and goggling, the tattoos seemed to come alive. In a panic, he twisted around. His back was covered, too.

He hunched over with his hands on his knees, then raced to the toilet and started to dry heave. Kneeling on the floor, he prayed aloud. "Please, oh please, God, let me be hallucinating!"

His practice and reputation would be ruined. His success now felt shameful and undeserved.

The doctor stepped into the shower and turned on the hot water. He stood beneath the scalding spray for as long as he could stand. Then he wrapped a towel around his waist and staggered back to bed.

Right before daybreak, he reached for the light switch on the lamp next to the bed. When he drew back his hand, he saw the tapestry of ink. Derek let out a strangled cry. Through the blurred veil of his tears, he saw the beautiful white tailored shirt and the pants he had worn to the award dinner lying crumpled on the floor. Picking them up, he searched the pockets and found the parking ticket from the hotel. The evening's events flashed back.

After the encounter with the hoodlums on the street, he'd driven around the hotel to collect himself. Just after he stepped out of the car, an old woman had approached. He couldn't understand what she was saying. A fog had seemed to encase him as he looked down into her painted face. Then a strange explosion had gone off inside his brain, drowning his senses. He'd felt her grabbing at his sleeve and desperately pushed her away. When he'd been able to see again, the old woman was lying on the ground.

I tried to help her. I did!

He remembered feeling startled and telling the doorman to take care of her. Giving the man some money and entering the hotel.

Derek rubbed his clammy forehead. Inside the banquet room . . . yes, that's when he started to feel sick. Like a green cloud of nausea that drained the energy from his body.

He remembered the valet coming over. It had seemed like an eternity before he returned with the car. Derek vaguely recalled slumping behind the wheel, exiting the hotel property, and turning out onto the street. It had taken everything he had to concentrate on the road. All he could think about was making it home into bed. He could still feel the relief of pulling his car into the parking garage. Then the long walk through the lobby of the building, past the security desk.

"The security desk!" Snapping back to the present, he reached for the phone. Derek choked back bile when he saw the inked fingers on his outstretched hand, then quickly hung up.

What had happened to him? He wondered if he was having another nightmare, but it was all too real. He forced himself to pick the phone back up and hit the two digits for the security desk.

"Security," a voice boomed out from the receiver. "Good morning, Dr. Hollinger, what can I do for you today?"

He swallowed. "Did you see anyone come up to my penthouse last night?"

"No, sir. Let me check the log." There was a pause. "Nope. Nothing registered for anyone coming or going since you came back in Saturday night."

He felt a chill. "What do you mean since I came back in Saturday night? What day is it?"

"What day is it, sir? Well, today is Monday, sir."

"Monday—"

"Yes, Monday." The guard's voice sounded strange. "Is there anything I can do for you, doctor?"

"No. Thank you." Derek severed the connection and sat down heavily on the edge of the bed. He looked at the clock. The red display said 5:36 a.m.

"I've been out for over thirty-two hours," he muttered, staring out the window in disbelief. A feeling of utter isolation and loneliness came over him. "Not a living soul has missed me. I could disappear off the face of the earth and no one would even notice."

He finally summoned the courage to return to the mirror and study his body. He was at least ten pounds lighter and illustrated with brightly colored tattoos from head to toe. "I'm unrecognizable," he whispered, fighting down a burst of panic.

A large dark blue dragon wrapped from his side up to his right pectoral muscle. He lifted his left arm to find the sinuous body of a black snake curling around the limb. His right arm had a crouching jaguar on the inner forearm. And on his back—three faces. One in particular riveted his terrified gaze, sending a wave of queasiness through his stomach. He would never forget it. *Could* never forget it.

The face of the man who had beaten him to within an inch of his life.

Derek drew a deep breath, studying the other tattoos. On his shoulder sat an angel. He touched the black and red spider on his neck. The legs wrapped around the base of his skull. What did it all mean? How could this possibly have happened? Sticking out his tongue, he saw it was now black. Not an inch of his body had been spared.

"How am I ever going to live a normal life again?" he cried.

He covered his face and started to sob.

"There must be some way to get rid of them," he muttered. "They can't be real!"

He shuffled to the kitchen and searched under the sink for abrasive powder, scrubbing at the ink on one palm and between his fingers. The image did not dissolve. He finally stopped when his skin began to burn and turn an angry red.

He examined the symbols on his knuckles. A message? A lion covered the top of his right hand. He looked closer to find intricate designs within the fur—yet none of it made any sense.

He dried his hands and went back to his bedroom.

Derek knew he kept people at arm's length while simultaneously demanding their absolute loyalty. He would emotionally sabotage himself and those around him. Somehow, the images inked all over his body seemed to reflect his damaged inner psyche, though he couldn't fathom how they had gotten there.

He sat down on the side of the tub. A chain wound around one of his ankles. *What significance could this possibly have?* He slid into miserable thoughts, until he heard a noise in the bedroom.

Derek stepped out of the bathroom. Standing with his crumpled tuxedo in her hand was a middle-aged Hispanic woman. His housekeeper, Cecelia.

Cecelia had been the cleaning woman through his younger years living with Dr. Casey. She had earned his trust through hard work and dedication. He paid her well so she worked only for him.

Now, she looked up to see a half-naked, entirely illustrated man. Cecilia let out a scream.

He held his hands out in a plea. "Cecelia, it's me, Dr. Hollinger."

She backed away, eyes wide. "No, no, you are not Dr. Hollinger! Get out, get out, or I'll call the police!"

"Okay, okay." He stepped back. "It's okay, it's all right."

"It's not all right," Cecelia cried. "You are not supposed to be here. Where is Dr. Hollinger?"

"I don't know. I think he's at work, I don't know. I'm leaving. I'm leaving right now!"

Derek grabbed a hooded sweatshirt from the hall closet. He dashed out the front door before she could scream again. Thankfully, the elevator was waiting. He leapt inside, then realized that in his haste, he'd left his wallet and phone on the dresser. He almost went back but decided against it. As the elevator door closed, he reached into his jeans pocket and felt his motorcycle key.

Chapter 3

Derek realized that the guard would spot him if he tried to access the parking garage, which was entered through the lobby. Instead, he slipped out the building's emergency exit. Used for deliveries, it was located around the corner from the elevator and out of sight of the security desk.

As he stepped into the alley, the gravity of the situation hit him hard. He'd distanced himself from childhood friends after the attack. Dr. Casey had been his only true companion and now he was gone. Derek jammed his hands into his pockets, walking aimlessly, thoughts slipping back twenty-five years ago . . .

The last day of school was a hot June afternoon, and the only thing on every kid's mind was going to the beach. His mother was coming home from work early. They planned to meet his grandmother, Carol, at the airport. Carol was his father's mother. They'd always been quite close, especially after his father's passing. They sat for hours while he listened to his grandmother tell stories and read from the Bible. They had forged a strong bond while they both grieved for the loss of a son and father.

But for young Derek, this was the worst possible day for her to arrive. Pool parties, beach parties, and everyone he knew was going to be there! The girl he had his eye on was going to be at one of them. Would he have another chance to see her through the summer? The last place a fourteen-year-old boy wanted to be is with his mother and grandmother on the last day of school.

The bell rang and the classroom doors burst open with an explosion of excitement as the students raced outside. With the echo of the slamming lockers through the halls, his feeling of dread escalated. He walked slowly to his locker to gather his things. *How could he get out of spending the day with his grandmother?*

The last of the lockers slammed shut. The loud voices subsided. Virtually alone now, Derek had stalled as long as he could. He stared out through the glass doors as he reached into the side pocket of his backpack, trying to think of a way to change the course of his immediate future. He pulled out a little wooden figurine he had carved in woodshop. It was an angel in remembrance of his father. He knew that his grandmother would cherish it.

But this was the last day of his first year of high school. He was ready to party. The dreaded freshman year was over. He and his buddies had not only survived, but they had thrived. They had become popular. This summer was just the beginning!

It seemed to Derek that his mother just didn't care about what *he* wanted. For the life of him, he could not understand her reason for picking this day of all days to bring his grandmother to town. Why would his mother do this to him? How could she be so thoughtless? Why couldn't she just look at things from his perspective? Didn't she care whether he was happy?

The weight of the world was on his shoulders as he stuffed the trinket back into his backpack. Derek pushed open the two large glass double doors, stepping out into the freedom of the beautiful summer day. He felt the searing sun on his face and neck. He stopped to pull his favorite cap from his backpack. His father had been an avid California Angels fan. He never left the house without the faded old red baseball cap.

He walked slowly, deep in thought, toward home four blocks away. How could he convince his mother that he should be able to skip this first day with his grandmother? How could he make it up to both of them?

As he thought about what his friends might be doing at the very moment, he heard the screech of tires come around the corner. He stopped in his tracks and looked up to see what the commotion was about. A small, red, foreign-made car braked hard right in front of him. All four doors flew open. Men ran toward him.

Derek froze in place as they swarmed around him. One had a devil tattoo on his neck and a spider web that covered the left side of his face. The right eye danced in the center of the web. Underneath sat the predatory spider.

With a malicious grin, he started to howl. Derek shuddered in fear, convinced that he was truly in the hands of the Devil.

A stick jabbed his stomach. Derek felt the air rush out of his body. Someone grabbed his arms from behind, while another punched his ribs. He took a blow to the arm—then heard a loud crack and felt excruciating pain as his leg broke. He stumbled and collapsed. Voices laughed through the barrage of blows.

As he lay on the sidewalk, he locked on the black, empty eyes of his attacker. The man was there to kill. Derek was now the prey caught in his web, staring into the face of death.

He watched in slow motion as the villainous arm went up. The stick whistled down and struck the side of Derek's head.

Darkness descended, like falling into his own grave.

Then his assailant reached down for the worn red baseball cap clinging to Derek's bloody head.

A trophy. A souvenir.

The predators laughed and high-fived as they took Derek's backpack with the carved angel meant for his grandmother. The car doors closed, one by one, and it sped off.

Derek's mother, Sandi, came home to an empty house. She had told Derek to be there right after school so they could get to the airport before his grandmother's plane landed.

His mom decided to backtrack his route home from school. She'd thought he might have stayed behind to hang out with his friends.

She watched the sidewalk as she drove. At the end of the first block, she noticed something strange. She couldn't make out what it was and slowed her car to see.

Derek's body lay in a crumpled heap in a puddle of blood. A red stream ran down the sidewalk. She jumped from her car, screaming his name.

Derek's grandmother, Carol, arrived at the hospital from the airport to find they had already taken Derek in for surgery. Sandi was seated in the waiting room when her former mother-in-law entered. Locking tear-filled eyes, the two women rushed into each other's arms. They had been here before when Derek's father lay dying of cancer. Sandi quickly brought Carol up to speed on the day's events.

The police had come, but since Derek was unconscious, Sandi could give them very little information.

After eight hours of surgery, the lead surgeon, Dr. Christopher Casey, came out to inform the family of Derek's status. It had been a very rough surgery with extensive tissue damage and multiple fractures. Worst of all, he had swelling on the brain and the doctors felt it best to induce a coma. Shutting down the functions of the brain gave it time to heal.

"How long will he be in a coma?" Sandi asked.

"We really don't know," Dr. Casey had replied.

"Is he going to have brain damage?" Carol asked in an anxious voice.

"The next couple of days are critical. We will continue to monitor his progress. This is a grave situation. We are going to make every effort to ensure that Derek comes out of this with the best results. Do you belong to a church or have some family or friends that you can call?"

"No, we haven't lived here long. It's just me and my son. I'm a widow. This is my deceased husband's mother who has come to visit."

The doctor put his hand on her shoulder and gave her a gentle squeeze. As he walked away, he couldn't help but feel her anxiety. He had once had a child himself.

For the next three days, Sandi and Carol sat by Derek's bedside while everything medically possible could be done to reduce the swelling of the brain. By the fourth day, the doctors tapered off on the medications used to induce the coma. Derek opened his one good eye, just long enough to acknowledge his grandmother. With the multiple traumas, the best line of defense was to monitor the patient in a lightly induced coma.

The two women felt a sense of relief that Derek had given them a positive sign of recovery. They decided they would start taking turns staying by his bedside. Each woman took her turn while the other rested. They talked to him and held his hand, making sure he knew one of them was always there.

Sandi decided that Carol should be the first to go home to rest, considering her frail state. It was apparent the violent attack on her grandson was taking a heavy toll on her. One afternoon, just as she was leaving, she collapsed in the hallway outside Derek's room. Hospital staff rushed her to the emergency room, but it was too late. Carol died of a massive heart attack.

She had lived just long enough to make sure her grandson would be okay.

Sandi chose not to tell Derek about his grandmother's passing when he was taken out of the coma. He did not remember that his grandmother had been there. He had also lost all memory of that day. Derek felt frustrated and angry, and suffered from fear and anxiety. He couldn't remember the content of his terrible nightmares when he woke in the morning with his hospital gown and bed sheets soaked in sweat.

Dozens of surgeries followed. The therapies for his speech and memory were a long and arduous process. Like a newborn baby, he had to learn to walk, talk, and even feed himself again. The road to recovery was slow and complex; the rehabilitation went on for years.

Derek's sophomore year came and went. None of his friends

came to the hospital anymore except for the kids that dropped by out of morbid curiosity. Derek felt trapped; unable to communicate. Then one day everyone except his mother stopped coming.

Derek had three surgeons just in the first year to reconstruct his face, eye, and nose.

Dr. Casey seemed to take a personal interest in Derek's rehabilitation. He brought books and spent a lot of time explaining the procedures. This is where the seed of Derek's interest in plastic surgery was planted.

Dr. Casey spent many days with Derek in the first few years of his rehabilitation. The old doctor would give Derek the encouragement he needed to continue physically and mentally. He realized that Derek was in dire need of an adult male figure who would take the time and energy to help develop him into a productive member of society.

When Derek became well enough to be released, the two had grown so close that, under very little protest from his mother, he moved in with the doctor. He still held his mother partially, if not wholly responsible for what had happened to him, and she willingly carried the guilt.

To relinquish her parental rights to a man of Dr. Casey's caliber was the least she could do to make amends to her son. The doctor genuinely loved Derek like a son, and she could only give them her blessing before she died.

The years passed and the doctor's complete dedication to Derek's recovery and development were apparent. He enrolled him in the local college. By the fourth year, he was ready for his pre-med classes. He sensed the love and dedication Dr. Casey had for his profession; he began to feel it, too. Dr. Casey continued to have a thriving reconstructive surgery practice in the heart of Los Angeles. He was Derek's surrogate father; his closest and only friend.

When Derek graduated from medical school, he went straight into practice with Dr. Casey. His mentor now had a successor.

Just ten years out of medical school, Derek inherited a successful business. He took on two partners to help with the workload and it became one of the biggest and most successful practices in Los Angeles.

Derek had no serious romantic relationships. The fear and insecurity he had felt growing up carried over to adulthood. He just couldn't put that kind of faith and trust into another person. The only people he had ever really cared about were gone.

Derek had lived vicariously through the old doctor. He had taken on the old doctor's passion and love for his craft. He had seen the world through the old doctor's eyes, and now he was continuing his legacy, just as Casey had meant it to be.

The business and practice of being a successful plastic surgeon were Derek's only focus in life, just as it had been with the old doctor—who died alone in the end, except for the relationship he'd built with Derek in his last surviving years.

He eventually remembered why he was on the sidewalk that fateful day. He also found out how his grandmother had passed away. The memories validated his hostile feelings. These traumatic events were put into motion by decisions his mother made. He blamed her for losing his high school years *and* his beloved grandmother.

Little did he know it wasn't over yet.

Derek staggered down the sidewalk. It was like the sun stood still. Time ceased to exist. An occasional stumble only intensified his struggle to stay lucid. The morning evaporated into bouts of paranoia.

He had become invisible to the other pedestrians. Just another homeless druggie.

With the drawstring of his hoodie pulled tight around his face, he relived Saturday night's events at the awards dinner and hotel again and again. Jamming his hand into his pants pocket, he felt the only tangible item linking him to his previous existence—a motorcycle key that he twirled between his fingers.

At last, he found himself outside his high-rise office building. He tilted his head skyward to look up to the top. He couldn't remotely begin to understand how he was on the verge of losing the entire world that he'd built.

I need help, he thought blankly, twisting the key in his trembling fingers.

Shuffling along, he contemplated each person that worked for him.

The doctor had no true friends. No one to rush to his aid, to help him untangle this mess. The only person who came to mind was Kendal Reed, his nurse and office manager.

Drawing his hood tighter, he skulked into the underground parking structure, locating the closest stairwell. He paused at the first landing, listening for voices. The ritual was repeated at each consecutive level, where he would pause to rest and keep an eye out for anyone who might catch a glimpse of his bizarre appearance.

The stairwell door opened slowly on the twentieth floor. He stepped into the hall, hugging the wall until he reached the double doors to his office. Pressing his ear flat against the wood, he heard only silence. But when he opened it a crack, faint voices came from deep inside the office.

He tiptoed across the alabaster marble floor, almost bumping into the black marble art deco-style table that sat in front of the trendy curved sofa. He paused in the hallway. His corner office door stood open, exposing the twentieth-floor view.

"Hey you, stop! Where do you think you're going?"

Recognizing the receptionist's voice, he turned slightly, feigning a cough from behind the hoodie. "Nicole, it's me, Dr. Hollinger. I'm not feeling well, please ask Kendal to come to my office."

"Oh! I'm sorry, doctor." She smiled. "I didn't recognize you. I'll get her right away."

He slipped into his office and collapsed against the heavy mahogany door. After a moment, he began to pace. The door flew open, catching him in midstride.

In the doorway stood Kendal's tiny frame. Her white lab coat was open, exposing light green scrubs. The office manager's dark ginger hair made her emerald eyes look even wider as she gasped and took a step back.

"Kendal, Kendal, it's me," Derek whispered. He pushed back his hood, throat tightening at the fear on her face. "It's me, Dr. Hollinger. It's me."

Her jaw dropped open at the familiar voice. Kendal studied him in astonishment. "What happened to you?"

She hurriedly closed the door. She'd recently redecorated the large executive office with eye-catching art and tropical plants to create a more relaxed atmosphere.

"I don't know!" Derek slumped against the mahogany pedestal desk.

"How can you not know?"

"I went to sleep," he said wearily, "and this is how I woke up."

She eyed him with obvious skepticism. "Well, something must have happened. Are the tattoos fake?"

He shook his head. "I tried scrubbing them off."

Kendal frowned. "You must have felt someone putting these tattoos on you. And this amount of work would take at least a year, wouldn't it?"

"I know." He gripped his disheveled hair. "It's all unbelievable. I can't understand how—or why—this would happen."

Kendal stepped forward and put her hand on his shoulder, eyes brimming with compassion. He realized she'd never seen him vulnerable before. He wore his status as a hotshot plastic surgeon like armor—and didn't let people get close.

"Has anyone seen you?" she asked.

"No one. Well, my housekeeper, Cecilia. She came in first thing this morning and caught me by surprise."

"A pretty big surprise," Kendal agreed. "She didn't recognize your voice?"

"No. She didn't seem to." He sighed dejectedly. "We were both shocked."

"Do you think she called anyone?"

"Who would she call?"

"You know, like the police."

"No, I don't think so. I thought about it after I left the penthouse. She's probably confused and doesn't know if the bizarre-looking person she saw is staying there or what. So I hope she waits until she talks to me." He blew out a breath. "Or the man I used to be."

"Have you called her?" Kendal asked.

"No." Derek chewed a nail. "Can you call her for me and just explain that I'm out of town?"

"Who do I tell her was in your penthouse this morning?"

"Tell her it was a friend and that I'll explain it to her when I get back home."

He wrote the phone number down on a pad. "She's been with me for years. She took care of my mentor Dr. Casey. She comes once a w—

"Don't worry, we'll figure this out." Kendal handed him a ginger ale from the small office refrigerator. "Now who else knows about this?"

"Nobody. Just you."

Kendal walked around to the back of his desk and put the call on speaker so he could listen. It rang several times and was about to go to voicemail when a woman's voice came on the line.

"*Hola.*"

"Cecelia?"

"*Sí.* Yes."

"This is Kendal. I work for Dr. Hollinger."

"*Sí.*"

"I am calling because Dr. Hollinger would like to know if you are okay."

Her voice went higher. "There was a man in the house this morning!"

They shared a look. "I know. Dr. Hollinger told me. He said the man scared you."

"*Sí*—I am so scared." She sounded close to crying. "I don't know what to do."

"You haven't called the police, have you?"

"No! No, police."

"Okay, Cecelia. Thank you. Dr. Hollinger will explain everything to you."

"I want to go home." She choked up. "I don't want to stay. Tell Dr. Hollinger I'm too scared to come back."

"Cecelia—wait—the doctor will explain everything."

"No. No. That was a very bad man that was here. That was an evil man. He comes because he is death."

Her words sent a shiver of ice down Dr. Hollinger's spine.

"Okay, Cecelia. The doctor will explain everything."

"*Sí*—Tell the doctor to call me." The phone went dead.

"She's pretty upset," Kendal said. "By the sound of her voice, I think your running out might have been the best decision. So what are you planning to do next?"

"Well, I know what I can't do. I can't let anyone here know—or let any of my patients know. Who would want to come to someone looking like me to make them look beautiful? I can't be seen." His jaw tensed. "I'd be ruined overnight."

"Well then, what do you propose to do?"

"I don't know. I really need some time to figure this out." He locked his fingers behind his head and drew in a hitched breath. "I don't know how this could happen, I must be able to go back and undo it."

They both turned at a knock on the door. "Dr. Hollinger?"

Kendal put her finger to her lips and motioned for the doctor to get behind the door. She came out from behind the desk and opened it.

"Did I hear Dr. Hollinger's voice?" It was Sandra, Dr. Lee's nurse.

"I was just listening to his messages," Kendal replied casually. "Did you need something?"

Sandra stepped forward. "He has a lot of patients looking for him."

Kendal was used to taking charge. She put her hand on the door jamb, blocking her path. "Sandra, the doctor is going to be on vacation for a few days. Ask Nicole to start calling his patients and let them know. Let's clear his schedule for the week."

Sandra stared in shock. "The whole week?"

"Yes, maybe next week as well. Tell the patients the doctor had a family emergency. Reschedule what you can with Dr. Brock or Dr. Lee. I am sure they will be happy to help."

She nodded slowly. "I didn't think Dr. Hollinger had any family."

"Extended family. Thank you, Sandra."

Kendal stepped back and closed the door firmly. The nurse lingered on the other side. A few seconds later, Sandra's footsteps could be heard retreating.

"That was quick thinking, but then that's why I hired you, right?" Derek said sarcastically, trying to be funny.

Kendal winced and reached for the brass door handle. "Let's get you out of here before she comes back."

"To where?" he wondered. "I can't go home."

She bit her lip as she looked over at him, where he was still hiding in the corner. "I suppose I can offer you my apartment for now."

Unable to express his gratitude, he diverted. "Let me grab a couple of things first."

Derek opened his desk drawer. Staring down at the contents, he realized there was nothing here he needed, nothing that would give him the answers he sought. He felt disconnected from the world around him. Dr. Hollinger, the wealthy, handsome success, felt like someone else entirely. Derek slid the drawer shut.

Kendal opened the door, looked past the Tiffany crystal wall sconce to the other end of the hall, and motioned for him to follow. They made it to the parking garage without being seen.

Once in Kendal's little red convertible, she tossed her white lab coat into the backseat and drove out of the garage. Then she set a jaunty fedora hat on her head. Auburn hair jetted out like rays of sunshine.

"Just what I need," Derek muttered. He scrunched down low in the passenger seat with his hooded sweatshirt tied securely around his head.

With Kendal, there was no hiding from the world. She glowed like a beacon. Everywhere she went, people noticed her. An electric, vibrant young woman, full of life and sprinting around town.

The drive was short. "This is the place." Kendal parked at the curb and jumped out to open one of the two massive decorative iron gates. Dr. Hollinger scanned the empty sidewalk, then quickly followed her into a courtyard.

Kendal smiled and pointed past a swimming pool to the second landing of an apartment complex. "That's where I live," she said proudly.

At the top of the stairs, she unlocked the front door and entered the living room, then opened the patio slider. An ocean breeze rushed in.

Kendal flipped a switch on the wall. A wicker ceiling fan started to spin. She glanced back at Derek, wariness in her face. She'd decorated the room with tropical plants and rattan furniture dressed in vibrant colored pillows and cushions. A mirror hung at the front door. In the corner of the room stood a big, covered cage.

"I like your place," he said awkwardly, all too aware of how critical he could be at work.

She seemed to relax a little. "Have a seat."

He chose a rattan chair as he watched her uncover the cage. The big white bird instantly came to life, running back and forth on his perch, bobbing his head up and down.

"This is Brutus. Brutus this is Dr. Hollinger."

"Derek," he corrected. "Call me Derek."

Brutus clicked and whistled as he paced back and forth. Then he let out a loud screech.

Derek winced. "Beautiful bird."

"Yeah, I love Brutus. He's my roommate and makes for a good alarm. I forgot to uncover him this morning. I was running a little late." She gave a weak laugh. "Don't tell my boss."

Derek didn't respond.

"Anyway, I was planning on coming back home at lunchtime. He doesn't like to be covered." She looked nervous. "Would you like something to drink? Soda, or some water?"

"I could use some water. The ginger ale helped a lot."

"You're probably dehydrated and hungry, too."

"I haven't even thought of food." He swallowed hard.

"When is the last time you ate something?"

"Um, sometime Saturday, before the award dinner."

"Saturday? That's two days ago! You have got to eat something." Kendal retreated into her tiny galley kitchen.

Derek's gaze wandered around the apartment. The living area and kitchen were separated by a breakfast bar. The kitchen had a small refrigerator, sink, and a tiny stove top, leaving very little counter space and even less for cabinets. He wondered if she entertained much, or had a boyfriend, but saw no sign of it. Kendal seemed to lead a solitary existence. Maybe they had more in common than they realized.

She pulled out some lunch meat from the refrigerator and set it on the countertop. Derek rose from the big rattan chair and moved to one of the small stools under the breakfast bar, watching her make his sandwich. "This place should be pretty easy to keep clean," he said, then suppressed a wince. It sounded snobby.

Kendal ignored the comment. "Do you think someone could have done this while you were drugged?"

"How could they get so much done? Unless there's new technology . . . But then why don't the tattoos look or feel fresh?"

He studied the charcoal gray clock and compass design imprinted on the top of his left hand.

"Have you tried to remove them?"

Agitated, Derek cracked his neck. "Yeah, of course. I scrubbed in the shower, then scrubbed with cleanser. Nothing changed. They're embedded in my skin."

"You mean like they came from the inside?"

"I don't know." He rubbed his temples. "I haven't thought about it that way."

She looked thoughtful. "I remember in one of the classes I took in college we discussed stigmata."

"What's a stigmata?"

"Well, they're marks, usually on the hands and feet, though they can be on other parts of the body, too." She eyed him seriously. "They're considered holy wounds, like those caused by the crown of thorns that Christ wore. The people who get them can be overwhelmed with emotion and sometimes pain."

"I can see why," he muttered bitterly, "especially if it ruined their lives."

"Um, I don't think that's it. A lot of these people were deeply religious or became deeply religious. St. Francis of Assisi is one of the most famous. If I remember correctly, St. Francis saw an angel that had been crucified. He was so moved by the experience it left wounds on his hands and feet. He even had the piercing in his side that would seep blood and soak his clothes. There are lots of stories like this."

Derek frowned. "I'm not a religious person, Kendal. My mom never took me to church. I've never had a reason to pursue such a subjective belief."

"I don't think it has anything to do with being religious," she replied calmly. "I remember in class we discussed that the link to these things could be dissociative disorders or identity disorders."

"Great." Derek gritted his teeth.

"Linked to post-traumatic stress syndrome," she continued, "expressed in unconscious self-mutilation."

Derek stood so fast the stool toppled over. "Are you saying that I did this to myself?" he demanded.

Startled, Kendal jumped, eyes wide and alert. "Not exactly! Look, you must have taken some of the same classes I did. You can speculate. Just think about it. Could there be something in your own past that connects to all this?"

Derek drew a deep breath. He picked up the stool and sat down, reflecting on his traumatic childhood. Part of him wanted to tell her everything, but he feared she'd pity him—view him as a pathetic victim.

"So when was the last time you felt normal?" Kendal asked.

"I guess the day of my award dinner. I got ready and drove over to the hotel."

"And you felt okay at the dinner?"

"No, not really. I'd just had a run-in with some teenagers on the street. They had me pretty worked up. I was feeling quite anxious." His stomach churned.

She looked confused. "Why didn't the chauffeured car pick you up?"

"I cancelled it. I wanted to drive my new Bentley. I was waiting for some teenagers to cross the street when a couple of them tried to jump in the car. Luckily, I was able to get away."

Kendal covered her mouth. "Oh, my goodness, did anyone get hurt?"

"I almost ran over a couple of them," he admitted. Blood rushed to his face. "But I don't care. I know they were all working together. I could tell by the way they watched while the other two tried to jack me."

His foot jittered against the floor. "I just gassed it. I ended up with a dent on the hood from one of those little thugs hitting it with his fist. When I got to the hotel I was still pretty shaken up. You know, from what had just happened. Then some old bag lady grabbed my arm. I didn't mean to push her down . . ."

"Wait." She tilted her head. "What do you mean?"

"I'm pretty sure she wasn't hurt," he said quickly. "It was all an accident! I was going to try to help her up until she pulled out a rattle and stared chanting in Spanish. When I saw that she was more angry than hurt, I entered the hotel."

Kendal refilled his glass of water while he tore his napkin into confetti. "What happened after that?"

"I went straight into the awards dinner." He pushed the napkin pile across the counter. "I started feeling kind of weird, like sick. So I didn't stay long. I didn't even get my award. I ended up going home early and going to bed. I thought maybe I was coming down with the flu or something. I was sick all night with terrible nightmares. It lasted through Monday when I woke up like this."

She stared at him. "I think maybe that old lady put a curse on you."

"A curse?" He shook his head in disbelief. "Are you kidding?"

"What else could it be?" she asked in a challenging tone.

"The idea that an old lady could do this just by . . . by *putting a curse on me* is pretty ludicrous."

"Let me make a few phone calls." Scrolling though her contact list, Kendal located the name of her psychology and behavioral professor. She left a message.

"I can't reach out to any of my colleagues," Derek said. "I don't have a phone." In a sullen voice he added, "I don't want anyone to know anyway."

Her professor called back almost immediately. He didn't know of anyone with specific training in post-traumatic stress disorders that had resulted in stigmata. But he did know a doctor of anthropology at UCLA. Kendal wrote down the information.

"Well, it's a start." She punched the numbers into her cell. "We can contact this doctor, explain the situation, and see where it leads us."

Derek shrugged. Exhausted, he stretched out across the couch. Before he could formulate a plan, he drifted off.

Chapter 4

While Derek slept, Kendal called the office and made sure the patients had been notified and the other doctors had been told of the "family emergency". Then she curled up in the oversized rattan chair with her laptop and started a search on stigmata.

She glanced over at the sleeping figure of her boss, then continued her internet search on tattoos and tattoo machines. Nothing came up that could account for the amount of ink work that had been done in such a short period of time.

She closed the laptop, bemused at the surreal turn her day had taken. Not just her day—her *life*.

Kendal had grown up in Taylor, Michigan. When she graduated high school, she decided to become a nurse. Kendal hated the snow. It was dirty and cold, and she missed the sun during the long winter months.

Her family life had been quite unstable. Her mother married three times, with the third husband as bad as the first. Through her teen years, she'd had to ward off these abusive sexual predators. They always tried to push the physical boundaries. All three had exhibited jealous and controlling behavior over her and her mother. Kendal had never felt safe in her own home. She never knew her father and never asked. The little bit she had heard was not good.

But she had a plan. Right after graduating nursing school, she took the money saved up from multiple jobs and bought a one-way airline ticket to escape to her mother's youngest sister, Sarah, who lived in California.

Aunt Sarah had always been supportive. She'd told Kendal that whenever she was ready, she could come and stay until she got on her feet. Kendal had always planned to take her up on her offer.

As Kendal's plane descended into LAX that first evening, she sat straight up in her seat, face pressed against the window. Lights sparkled below as the aircraft broke through the clouds. She had never seen anything quite so magnificent as the way the landscape was covered in a blanket of lights as far as the eye could see. This was the beginning of her new, exciting life with no past, just a future to be written any way she chose.

She collected the two pieces of luggage that held all her worldly possessions and stepped out into the hustle and bustle of the city night. She could smell the cool ocean air and sense it had been a hot day by the way the heat fogged up from the pavement.

Looking up to study the different types of transportation signs, she breathed in deep and thought, *The air didn't smell like this in Michigan.*

Cars, buses, and shuttles zoomed past as she looked for the name of the shuttle that would take her to the bus stop. Her aunt had provided her with detailed instructions on how to catch the shuttle and get to the bus that would bring her to the house. It was almost midnight by the time she arrived; the lights were on as she stepped up to the door and knocked lightly. The door opened almost immediately. There stood her Aunt Sarah with open arms and a big smile on her face. Kendal knew in her heart she had made it home.

The next morning, still consumed with excitement for her future, she took an early walk to the market. The morning was clear and bright with the sun already intense. Kendal realized it was only hot when standing directly in the sun and made the two-block hike quickly. Motivated to find a job and an apartment, she had decided to get an early start to purchase the morning newspaper. In no way did she intend to take advantage of her aunt's generosity.

With a newspaper in one hand and a cup of coffee in the other, Kendal found a table outside on the sidewalk with an umbrella for shade. Sipping her morning brew, she turned straight to the want-ads section to see what was happening in the local market. Her focus on the paper did not last long. She found it hard to concentrate with the whirlwind of activity.

People walked little dogs and big dogs, and even a cat on a leash. They pushed dogs in strollers, jogged into the coffee house with headphones plugged into their ears, or rode up on bikes.

There was such a buzz, it was amazing that the people had so much energy and zest so early in the morning. L.A. was a complete reversal of the environment from which she had just come. Everyone here seemed so full of life; they walked and moved with purpose. Kendal felt like she had been dropped off on a happier, more energetic planet.

As hard as it was to keep her concentration, by midmorning she had completely scoured the job ads. She needed to get back to her aunt's house before she started to worry.

When Kendal arrived, Aunt Sarah was sitting at the kitchen table, dressed and ready to go.

"Ah, good morning! There you are." She stood from the table. "I was hoping you would be back in time to go to the doctor with me today."

"You're going to the doctor?" Kendal repeated. "Is there something wrong?"

"Oh, no. It's just a minor procedure." She smiled assuredly. "I'd appreciate a ride home afterward."

"Of course! I'd be happy to drive. Just give me a couple of minutes to get ready."

"No rush. We still have plenty of time."

By the time Kendal took her shower and returned, her aunt stood in the middle of the kitchen with purse and car keys in hand.

With the traffic, the drive downtown took about forty-five minutes. Kendal followed her aunt's directions and pulled into a parking structure that appeared to be connected to a high-rise building. She parked the car and walked across the garage to the nearest elevator. Kendal pushed the button and the elevator doors opened immediately; they both stepped inside. She looked at the row of buttons. The building had thirty floors! She watched her aunt push the button for the twentieth floor. The doors closed in front of them.

It seemed to take a full minute for them to reach the twentieth floor. Kendal could not remember ever being in a building that high. When the doors opened, her aunt stepped out and turned to her left. Kendal followed closely as they walked to the end of the hall where there were two large double doors. Her aunt pushed opened one of the doors as Kendal reached over to assist. Once inside, they were transported into another world. The nondescript commercial look disappeared into plush, spa-like decor.

They stood waiting in the tranquil room in front of a shiny black and brown marble-topped desk as Kendal visually assessed the waiting area; on the alabaster floor sat an elegant mahogany-framed red leather couch and chair with a black pearl granite side table. The room smelled of rich botanical scents you would find in a beauty spa.

Kendal was beginning to think that maybe her Aunt Sarah had made a mistake. It didn't seem like a medical office. She was about to double-check when a young woman walked to the front desk and asked her aunt which doctor she was there to see.

"Dr. Hollinger," Sarah replied.

The receptionist turned and asked Kendal's aunt to follow. She then handed the two women over to what appeared to be a nurse by her uniform, who then escorted them to a small consulting room. The nurse had Kendal's aunt sit on a table and motioned for Kendal to sit in a chair. She pulled out a computer screen that hung against the wall and started typing on the keyboard mounted below the screen. She asked a few questions and took Aunt Sarah's vitals.

"The doctor will be in to see you shortly," she said cheerfully, bustling away.

Almost immediately, there was a light tap on the door. In walked a young, good-looking doctor who seemed friendly but formal.

"Good morning, ladies. Are you ready to go?" Dr. Hollinger asked Sarah.

"Yes, Dr. Hollinger. I am," Sarah responded without hesitation.

"I can't wait to get this over with. I am so embarrassed, I can't even wear my hair up anymore."

Upon saying that, she pulled back her hair. To Kendal's surprise, more than half of her aunt's left ear was missing. Sarah had told Kendal that she had to have part of her ear removed because of a malignancy, but Kendal had no idea how bad the tissue damage was.

The doctor stepped forward and proceeded to examine the small piece of flesh that was left on the side of her aunt's head.

"We are going to do what is called an auricular reconstruction. As we discussed in the past, we'll need to do a couple of surgeries to complete the reconstruction."

Once Dr. Hollinger finished explaining the procedure, he looked over at Kendal for what seemed to be the first time. Without any acknowledgment, as if still deep in thought, he turned toward the door.

"I'll check on you again after the surgery. I promise, you're in good hands." With that statement, he left the room.

Aunt Sarah smiled and re-covered her partial ear with her hair.

"I'm glad you're here, Kendal. This is a little scary. The first surgery to remove the malignancy was very scary, but I knew it was necessary to save my life. This surgery is more about the quality of life. I don't want to have to worry about anyone seeing my disfigurement. It bothers me all the time," Aunt Sarah confessed.

Kendal squeezed her hand. "Then I'm happy you're getting your ear rebuilt. I'll be here for however long you need me."

The door opened and the nurse said to Aunt Sarah, "Are you ready to go? We have a room ready for you."

Aunt Sarah was shown to a changing room. Kendal was shown back to the outside waiting area.

Kendal made herself at home. She had never been in such a luxurious environment, and she was enjoying it immensely. The receptionist continued to check with her periodically to see if she needed anything to drink—tea, coffee, water. She read a couple of magazines, imagining herself as a wealthy woman of leisure. The fantasy was short-lived.

The next time Kendal saw her aunt was after the surgery a couple of hours later. She was called back to the little room where they had moved her aunt to recover from the anesthesia. When Kendal walked into the room, Sarah was still out cold, her skin ashen. Right away, Kendal knew this was a worrisome sign.

Her oxygen levels must not be too good, Kendal thought.

She walked straight over to the monitors. Her aunt's blood pressure was very low. The nurse had left when Kendal arrived. *Where did she go? And what was taking her so long?*

Kendal started to talk to her aunt, asking her to wake up. Asking her if she could hear her. There was no response. Again, Kendal checked the monitors. Sarah's blood pressure continued to drop. She was in trouble. Kendal ran into the hall just as alarms went off on the machines. Her aunt had stopped breathing.

Kendal hurried back to her aunt's bedside. Saw an emergency call button on the side of the bed and hit it as the blood pressure monitor continued to chime. She started chest compressions and mouth-to-mouth. The nurse came rushing back into the room.

"Get the doctor!" Kendal gasped in between compressions. The nurse turned on her heels and ran out of the room.

Kendal continued to give her aunt mouth-to-mouth resuscitation for what seemed to be an eternity. She could hear voices and running feet. Finally, the doctor slid in beside Kendal and started to work on her aunt. A push of the I.V. and her aunt's heart began to beat again. Her vital signs gradually returned to normal. Sarah opened her eyes. A big sigh of relief went around the room.

The doctor motioned to Kendal and asked if he could speak to her outside. She hesitated, reluctant to leave her aunt.

"Don't worry, she's being watched very closely now," he said. "She is going to be fine."

Kendal accompanied the young doctor down the hall to his office. He walked around a beautiful mahogany desk and sat down in a big leather-bound chair.

"Have a seat." He motioned to one of the oversized leather chairs that sat in front of his desk.

"I'd rather not," Kendal replied curtly.

"How do you know so much about medical emergencies?" The doctor leaned back in his chair, studying her.

"I was—I *am* an E.R. nurse."

"Really?" the doctor said with surprise.

She bristled. "What do you mean, *really*?"

"Oh, well, just by looking at you I would never have guessed."

"Why?" She frowned. "What does an emergency room nurse look like here in California?"

"That's not what I meant—"

"What *did* you mean?"

"I don't know." He shrugged. "You look so young."

Her irritation faded. "Well then, I guess I'll take that as a compliment."

"Where do you work?"

"I don't have a job."

He eyed her with surprise. "Why not?"

"I just came to town," she explained. "I'm still looking around."

"I have an opening if you're interested."

Her brows rose. "I don't know. Things seem pretty lax around here."

He didn't look offended. "My thoughts exactly," Dr. Hollinger agreed. "I could use someone like you. Someone who isn't afraid to step up and take matters into her own hands. I work with two other doctors so we're constantly busy." He smiled. "Kind of like an ER."

Kendal didn't smile back. She wasn't sure if she liked this guy or not. "Can I think about it?"

He nodded. "Send me your resume. Let's set an appointment for a couple days from now after your aunt is feeling better. You can come back in with her for her check-up, let me know then if you are interested. How about that?"

The doctor got up from his desk and walked over to Kendal, who was still standing by the door. He motioned for her to step out into the hall and led her back to the room where her aunt lay resting comfortably.

A month later, Kendal moved into her own apartment. Most people in the complex used the barbeque area by the pool on weekends, and it wasn't long before she befriended her neighbors and it truly became home.

Dr. Hollinger had been very persuasive, offering a nice salary with a signing bonus. One of her patients had told her about this apartment complex. Everything had fallen into place.

She used her first paycheck to move in. The landlady Mrs. Harris, being a kind old soul, let her skip the security deposit. Mrs. Harris never hesitated to call on her any time she felt a little under the weather. It was an unspoken understanding between the two of them that she had done Kendal a favor. Kendal liked having the old lady depend on her a bit. It made her feel more welcome. Like she truly belonged there.

The massive gates opening into the courtyard worked out quite well since Kendal liked to park her convertible right out front on the street. Everyone else in the complex had a carport. Her apartment had been a little cheaper because of the inconvenience, which had helped her in the first year. But by the second year she had grown quite used to the arrangement.

When it did finally rain, Kendal was happy to see it rain in California, too. Nothing could dampen her spirits. She loved the California weather and lifestyle.

It took two months for Kendal to transform physically, mentally, and emotionally from a plain Michigan girl to the bright and happy California girl.

Kendal now sported shoulder-length ginger red hair. She no longer wore the drab, long brown hair that she had come out to California with. She loved to wear hats. She sported a hat most of the time, with her auburn hair jetting out from underneath. Her favorite was her fedora. She pierced her nose and ears and got a tattoo of a sun on her ankle.

The changes unnerved Dr. Hollinger—and he never missed an opportunity to let her know it.

But Kendal was living the dream. Her dream, the California

dream. She didn't care what anyone thought or said, not even Dr. Hollinger—though sometimes his criticisms did hurt.

At first, the doctors had been quite pleased with her performance. They had shown their approval by rewarding her financially. She worked well with the other nurses, who had neither the knowledge nor the desire to take on the position that Kendal had stepped into.

But Dr. Hollinger always had some smart comment to make about her hair or about her tattoo. He especially gave her a hard time about the nose ring when she first got it. She decided to keep a very small diamond stud so as not to be too noticeable, since she knew it bothered him.

Lately, she'd been coming in early to ensure everything in the operating rooms was ready to go. But instead of noticing all her hard work, Dr. Hollinger had continued his barrage of snide comments. She wasn't sure where it came from. He depended on her for everything.

When he showed up at the office, covered in tattoos, she could hardly believe it. Another person might have left him to fend for himself—especially after the way he'd treated her—but Kendal had a big heart. And she'd always suspected that part of her boss's snarkiness masked personal insecurity.

Now, Dr. Hollinger . . . *Derek* . . . began to toss and moan. She tried calling his name, then tapping his arm as his cries became louder. Finally, she grabbed his shoulder and shook.

"Are you okay?"

His eyes flew open. He sat up, blinking rapidly. "Yeah, I think so."

"What had you so upset?"

"I'm not sure." He ran tattooed fingers through his hair. "I think I was back at my old high school. I've had this dream before."

"Do you think this is connected to drugs?"

"Drugs? No, it doesn't feel like drugs."

"I'm thinking someone gave you some kind of hallucinogen."

"Yeah, but I don't think it could make me manifest a body full of tattoos. Unless you know about a drug that I don't."

"No." She sat down next to him. "It was just a thought. You have so many different conditions going on. It might not be just one thing. Where were you last night?"

"I told you, I was home." He jumped up and started to pace. "The last time I went out was Saturday night. I had the award dinner at the New Century Hotel in Los Angeles. I knew just about everyone there. I can't think of anyone that would want to drug me. I mean why would they? Right?"

"I don't know. What did you do before the award dinner?"

"My normal routine. I got up Saturday morning, went downstairs to the gym, then took a ride to the beach on my motorcycle. I came back, hung out at the pool, and got a massage. I think I did some work in my office, took a shower, got ready, and went to the award dinner."

"Nothing else happened?"

"Like I said, there was the run-in I had with the teenagers, then later the old woman at the hotel."

"Explain the run-in with the kids and the old woman again."

"Sorry." Clenching his jaw, he continued. "Well, I was dressed in my tuxedo. I jumped in my car to go over to the hotel. I left the window down because it was such a nice day. I was listening to the music, not really paying attention to what was going on. Then I came to a crosswalk with some teenagers. I was watching them. They were really starting to aggravate me when a couple of them came from behind."

He walked to the window, staring out. "I hit the gas. One of them hit the hood of my car. It left a dent. Before I knew it, I was at the hotel. Still shaken up. So I drove around the block. When I got out of the car this old woman came up to me. I tried to ignore her. She grabbed my arm and I remember feeling a sharp pain in my head. I couldn't see, I reacted and flung my arm up, which caused her to fall back. I tried to help her, but she grabbed a rattle and started shaking it and chanting in Spanish. I figured there was nothing I could do, so I just went on inside the hotel."

"What did this woman look like?"

"She was old. Maybe in her late seventies or early eighties. I think she had black hair with gray streaks. She had a tattoo on her face and her arm." His eyes narrowed. "Oh, my God! The tattoo . . ."

"You said she was chanting and screaming at you, right?"

"Yeah, she had that thing in her hand, like a rattle or something."

Kendal crossed her arms. "Like I said, I think . . . Maybe she was putting a curse on you."

"But I don't believe in that stuff!"

"Well, maybe you should look in the mirror."

Derek sighed. "You really think she could have the power to do something like this?"

"I don't know, but I think we should find out. Don't you?" She paused. "I have a kickboxing class to go to tonight. Would you like to tag along?"

Monday and Wednesday nights were kickboxing nights. She had a group of friends that she sparred with on a regular basis, all men and married except for one or two. They were like big brothers, teasing and keeping an eye out for her when it got rough.

"No. I don't want to go out. I still don't have much energy and I don't want to be seen like this."

"Will it bother you if I go?"

"I'm not here to disrupt your life."

"Do you want me to pick up something to eat on my way back?"

"No. The sandwich helped."

"Okay, I still think you need to eat something else. I'll be back in a little bit. Just make yourself at home." Kendal turned. "Brutus." The sound of his name made the bird run back and forth along his perch. "Keep Dr. Hollinger company."

"Derek," he reminded her.

"Derek." She smiled. "Keep Derek company."

Picking up her gym bag, Kendal headed out, leaving Derek to his thoughts.

⁂

"What if that were true?" he muttered to himself. "What if that old lady had the power to put a curse on me? I would have to find her and make her take this curse off. She has to want something. Money? She was panhandling."

He opened the laptop on the breakfast bar, sat down on the barstool, and typed in the word "curse". Downloads for games were at the top of the list. He went to the online dictionary. "A curse is an expression which comes from adversity or misfortune that will befall or attach itself to some other entity."

This is like reading my fortune. He had experienced more than his share of adversity in his life.

He clicked on the next link: "A curse may refer to a witch that harms or will inflict a spell, a prayer, magic, or witchcraft, by any supernatural powers, through a god, natural force, or a spirit. The accompanying ritual is considered to have some causative force in its result."

He flashed back to the old woman and how she reacted to him pushing her away. Chanting and shaking a rattle as if she were performing some sort of spell or witchcraft.

"That's it!" He slammed the laptop closed, shaken. "That old woman put a curse on me."

Chapter 5

Kendal was aware of how her involvement with Derek triggered her childhood abuse defense mechanisms. She was determined not to let his trauma affect her emotions or her hard-won sense of self. But she felt like she owed him, too, despite his shortcomings. He had given her the start she needed in California and had taken very good care of her financially.

Despite the weird day, Kendal arrived at the gym in a cheery mood. The boss that had made her life so miserable was now the new, vulnerable Derek. The kickboxing class was her therapy—a good cardio workout to relieve the stress.

"Hey, Kendal, are you going for a quick beer?" one of the guys called out. "After class?"

"I can't," Kendal replied getting up from the floor after doing her cool-down stretches. "I have an unexpected houseguest I have to get back to."

"Oh!" sang the chorus.

The three younger, smaller guys seemed to look up to the two older, larger guys as they laughed and hit each other on the arms. They were their own little kickboxing gang. She found them amusing.

"Joe, how's your nose healing?"

Joe gave a flexed muscle wave. "Real good, you did a fine job. Did you have family fly in or something?"

"No, I wish. Nothing like that." Kendal smiled at the group of misfit kickboxers. "It's the doctor I work for. He's having some personal problems and I'm just helping him out."

"Really?" Joe smirked. "Is the old ball and chain giving him a hard time?"

The group laughed in unison.

Kendal smiled. "No. it's nothing like that. He's never been married. At least I don't think he has. I don't think anyone would want to marry this one. He's a real downer type, if you know what I mean?"

"Then why are you mixed up with him?" Joe seemed bothered; Kendal suspected he'd always had a bit of crush on her.

"He's my boss. He asked me to help." She shrugged. "What am I supposed to do?"

Joe stepped up close. "Listen Kendal, if you need any help, you just let me know," he said in a low voice.

Kendal moved away with a neutral smile. "Thanks guys, that's really nice of you, but don't worry, I definitely have this one under control."

Joe looked dejected—and a little angry—as she picked up her bag and waved to the rag-tag group, then walked out of the gym. A few minutes later, she entered the apartment and found Derek sitting at the bar working on her laptop.

"Find anything?"

"Yeah." He met her gaze levelly. "I do think I have a curse on me."

Kendal raised her eyebrows. She opened the refrigerator and grabbed a cold bottle of water, then rolled it across her forehead and leaned back against the sink. "Kind of hard to believe someone can put a curse on you and get these kinds of results though."

Derek put his head in his hands, then scratched his head hard and looked up at Kendal's flushed face. "What else could it be? What else could create this kind of turmoil?"

"I don't know." She took a sip of water. "I'll call that professor at UCLA again in the morning. At least that's somewhere for us to start, right?" She suddenly remembered. "Oh my goodness, I was supposed to pick up something to eat!" She put the cap back on the water bottle. "Now I guess we'll just have to go out."

He scowled. "I can't go out."

"Why? I can barely recognize you, and I work with you every day."

Derek stared into the rattan-framed mirror that hung in the entry. "You're right." He touched the dollar bill in the shape of a tear drop below his eye. "Okay, I'm starved. Let's do it."

"Just wait a minute. I'll be right back." Kendal changed out of her workout gear, grabbed her keys off the counter, then side-stepped him. "Lock the door behind you," she said as if everything were normal, putting her fedora on her head.

Kendal's car sat right outside the gate with the convertible top down. She jumped into the driver's seat and smiled up at Derek standing outside the car. "What do you feel like?"

He opened the passenger door and slid down into the tiny car. "You pick."

The blinking open sign shone bright in the dark window when they pulled into the dirt parking lot of the small Mexican restaurant. The old Spanish-tiled building looked like it had been around since the turn of the previous century.

"Don't be scared." Kendal said, as she held open one of the heavy wooden doors. "It has great authentic food."

Derek stepped into the dark. "I bet it does."

A couple sat at the massive wooden bar. The booths had tall backs, making it hard to tell if there were any other patrons. It occurred to Derek that the privacy and dim lighting were why she had picked this place. Seemingly out of nowhere, a waiter appeared with menus in his arms.

Kendal stepped forward. "Two."

He led them to the back of the restaurant and laid the menus down in one of the high-backed booths. "Something to drink?"

Sliding into the seat, Kendal said, "Water for me."

"I'll have a beer," Derek answered.

"What kind of beer would you like?"

"Whatever you have on tap." Derek picked up a menu. "I need something to help me sleep. Beer always makes me sleepy."

The man came back with their drinks and they both ordered.

Kendal had no idea how to have a normal conversation with a man who for the past two years had ridiculed her with snide remarks about her hair, jewelry, and anything else that he could torture her with.

Derek broke the silence. "What if I stay like this the rest of my life?" He sipped the beer. "I just can't imagine . . . My career will be ruined, my life will be over."

"Don't say that." Kendal reached out to touch his tattooed hand. "As long as you have your health, there is hope for things to get better. Things could be a lot worse."

With anger in his eyes, he yanked his hand back and slapped the table. Kendal jumped.

"You really didn't just say that? You naïve girl! *Could be worse.* Listen, I have already been through *the worst.* I have come out of a coma, had my whole face reconstructed, had to learn to walk and talk again after almost being beaten to death. To have to go through this crap at this stage of my life . . ." His shoulders slumped. The fight went out of him. "I don't know if I can make it through this. I don't know if I have the strength to fight something this big again. I was almost beaten to death when I was a kid."

Kendal stared in shock. "Who would do that to a child?" she asked softly.

"It was the last day of my freshman year in high school. I was supposed to walk home after school. My mom had made arrangements with my grandmother to have her come out to visit. She was going to be flying in that day. So I had to get home to go with my mom to pick her up. I tried to get out of it, but my mom insisted I had to be with her at the airport when my grandmother arrived."

"Why?"

"Because . . ." He stretched his neck. "My grandmother was my dad's mother. She took care of me after he passed. Mom felt obligated. She was coming to see *me.*"

"Oh, I see."

"I really wanted to see her. But I wanted to be with my friends more. After school, I stalled for as long as I could, hoping to come up with an idea to get out of going to the airport. By the time I was done messing around, the school was pretty much empty. I was walking home really slowly, stalling for time when, all of a sudden, this car screeches up right in front of me. A bunch of guys jump out. They were all older and quite a bit bigger than me. They looked like they were part of a gang or something. They all had shaved heads with tattoos and piercings. They were really scary looking."

"You had never seen these guys before?"

"Nope, had never seen them before, or ever again. The ringleader had a tattoo, a spider web that circled the left side of his face. His eye was like in the center of the web and the spider was below his eye. These were some pretty twisted individuals."

"Why would they want to hurt you?"

"Because they could. Maybe it was an initiation, or they were out joy riding and wanted to kick some poor slob's ass. The police never found them."

She leaned forward. "So what happened to you?"

"Well, they beat me senseless. They broke just about every major bone in my body—my jaw, nose, shoulder, ribs, arm, and leg. Even my eye socket. It gave me a brain trauma. I ended up missing the rest of high school. I lost all my friends, everything that mattered to me."

"I'm so sorry."

He looked away. "That's not the worst part."

"No?"

"While I was in a coma, the stress of it all killed my grandmother right there in the hospital."

Kendal covered her mouth. "Oh, no."

"I never got to see her. My mom didn't even tell me. So, when I came out of the coma, I had no clue what had happened. She didn't want to upset me. I had a serious brain injury, so my memory was pretty messed up for a long time."

"I'm so sorry, Derek."

"I know. I feel like someone is out to get me. Why should I have to keep putting up with such lousy things happening in my life?"

"I don't think that's what's going on here."

"Oh, just what I need now." His fists clenched. "You telling me how I feel."

She looked exasperated. "That's not what I'm trying to do."

"So now what?" His voice was tight. "Maybe you're starting to feel a little sorry for me?"

"I don't feel sorry—"

"Well, I certainly don't need pity from someone like you!"

"Whoa! What does that mean?"

"It doesn't matter," he muttered, regretting his childish outburst. "It's happened now. I have to fix it. I'm not going to stay this way. People are either going to pity me or look at me in disgust. Either way, I'm pretty much screwed. But I'm not going to settle for it."

"Well, then." She sat straight back in the booth. "I think you should start by finding out what the probability of this being a curse is and what you have to do to reverse it."

"Reverse it?" he asked with cautious hope.

"Yeah, reverse it. I'm sure there must be a way to take a curse off."

Kendal had lost her appetite and motioned for the bill.

"Keep track of everything you spend. I'll make sure I get the money back to you first chance I get," Derek said.

"Oh, I intend to." She smiled. "Come on, let's go. We have a big day tomorrow."

The vivid, disturbing dreams returned that night. He tossed and turned on Kendal's couch. It was driving him insane. Every time he tried to sleep, the demons came rushing in. During the day, he felt like he was wired with anxiety.

By the time the sun rose, he was already up and sitting out on the patio.

Chapter 6

Derek was having his second cup of coffee when he heard the bedroom door open. He stood to peek inside the sliding glass door.

Still half asleep, with hair disheveled, Kendal shuffled toward the tiny kitchen. "What are you doing?" she asked.

"Having coffee. There's more in the kitchen."

"Yeah, that would be nice," she muttered.

He chuckled; he had no idea Kendal was not a morning person. She always appeared so chipper in the morning at work. He sat back down and waited for her to appear.

Derek watched in amusement as she wandered out wearing a pair of old, faded sweatpants and an oversized T-shirt. She fell into the chair holding a "Greatest Place on Earth" mug.

"Did you sleep?" She covered a yawn with the back of her hand.

"Yeah, I got some."

Staring into space, she took a sip of her coffee. "I love this place in the morning. It is so quiet. I love to sit out here and watch the sun come up."

He smiled. "You mean you've actually done this before?"

She pushed a lock of auburn hair back from her forehead. "Yes. I have done this before."

The neighbor's palm tree shaded the balcony perfectly as the sun became brighter.

"Let's drive over to the college this morning," she suggested. "Maybe we can catch the professor between classes."

"That's a good idea. But I need to take a shower, if that's all right with you?"

"Of course. We should probably go by your penthouse and get some clothes today."

"I think you had better do that. I'll call the security desk to give them my code so they can let you in."

Kendal got up from her chair and went inside. She returned a little while later with a stack of green scrubs in her hand. "Here you go." She tossed them over to Derek. "One of these should fit."

He picked up the pile. "I won't take too long."

"Towels are in the cabinet. I'll head over to your penthouse. But first you'd better make a quick call to the security desk."

Derek stopped in Kendal's bedroom and grabbed her cell phone off the dresser. Luckily, one of the regular security people was on duty. He explained the situation and asked the security guard to make a note. He then stepped into the small bathroom and closed the door. He hadn't had an opportunity to look at the rest of his body since that first morning.

It was unnerving to see the illustrations from head to toe again. He took the hand mirror to look from behind. His buttocks were tattooed with a ship sailing on blue and green waves that covered the entire cheek. The other cheek was a war scene. A man stood looking up at black planes bombing electrical towers with red flames in the background. Across Derek's lower back appeared to be a colorful jungle scene with parrots, tangled vegetation, trees, and tropical flowers. A jaguar could be seen prowling out from a bush.

While Derek was studying his tattoos in the bathroom, Kendal finished getting ready in her bedroom. She could hear the shower running and wondered if his entire body was covered. She listened for a minute at the door. Then she grabbed her keys and knocked. "Okay, I'm leaving now. I'll be back in a little bit. Do you have an alarm system?"

"Oh, yeah." He quickly wrapped a towel around his waist.

The bathroom door swung open. Kendal's face warmed. She felt a small jolt of electricity. Derek Hollinger had the best set of abs she had ever seen—even with the tattoos. She tried to avert her eyes.

"Here," he said, oblivious to her reaction. "I'll write it down for you."

Kendal stepped back. She could see the faces of three men on his back. An angel sat on his upper right shoulder.

"Who are the men?" she asked.

"I think those are the guys who beat me." He shook his head.

"What?" Her brow furrowed in disbelief.

"These tattoos seem to have some kind of meaning; I just need to figure it out."

"Wow, that makes it even weirder." She frowned. "I'll be back soon. Then we'll go over to the college and see if someone can help us figure it out."

Derek tightened the towel around his waist. "The alarm may or may not be set. So be careful. Cecelia never sets it when she leaves. But you should have the code just in case."

"Where are your keys?" She glanced at the towel.

"Oh, yeah, no keys. Have security let you in. Grab my wallet and phone, too. On my dresser."

Derek stood in the bedroom half-naked until he heard the front door close.

With the overwhelming feeling of being alone, he went back into the bathroom and shut the door. His image no longer visible in the steamed-up mirror, he stepped into the shower and started soaping down while examining the artwork that covered his legs, calves, arms, and torso.

He noticed Kendal's razor on the ledge. On impulse, he grabbed the hand-mirror and propped it up on the shelf. He lathered his head and started to shave. The hair began to fall in big clumps to the shower floor. He rinsed the last of the soap off. He could now see the illustrations on his head.

He dried off. Wiped down the steamed-up mirror. Then he gathered the hair from the shower and flushed it down the toilet. He opened the bathroom door to let the steam out, wiped the mirror again, then stopped to study the large black heart that covered the left side of his chest. Just looking at it made his eyes water. He could feel the darkness and loss of all those he had loved in his life.

The scrub bottoms fit a little tight. He went back through the living room passing Brutus talking inside his cage, then out to the patio deck. He started thinking back on his life. His childhood had started out happy. His father spent a lot of time with him. He was a patient and loving parent. And his mom had provided a stable home. Everything changed when his father became sick, the cancer ravaging his body.

Deep in thought, he heard Kendal return carrying a large piece of luggage.

"I grabbed a few things I thought you would need."

"Thank you," he said gratefully. "Did anyone say anything to you?"

"The security guard gave me the key. I think everyone was still asleep."

"Didn't security stop you when you came in the door?"

"No ..." Kendal's gaze wandered down his bare chest, then jerked back to his face. Her cheeks were pink. "Uh, yes. Sorry. When I got there. He had me sign the sheet."

"Great. That really makes me feel secure." He flung the suitcase on the couch and opened it.

Kendal was staring at him oddly. "I like the new look."

"Oh yeah." Derek ran his hand across his shorn skull. "Didn't miss a spot."

She blushed again. "I guess I'll let you get changed."

She back-pedaled her way into the bedroom, shutting the door. If Derek didn't know better, he'd think . . . well, that she might be attracted to him. But how could it be possible? He looked like a freak! And Kendal was his office manager. He had never really noticed her in that way before. But she had a great laugh. She was kind and intelligent—

"I think we should head over to the college!" she called through the bedroom door.

He tried to focus. "That sounds like a good idea." Derek pulled a white V-neck T-shirt over his head. "I'm ready!"

Kendal walked out of the bedroom wearing a floral sundress.

Derek stopped to admire the bright colors against her tanned, athletic body. He had always seen her as a disciplined nurse with dyed hair and a nose piercing. He watched her pick up her purse.

She stood with the front door open. "After you," she said with a cheeky smile.

He waited at the bottom of the stairs while she locked the door. One of the neighbors across the courtyard was looking out the window.

"Kendal." He motioned over to the window. "I think we have company."

Kendal smiled and waved. "Good morning, Mrs. Harris."

Her neighbor gave her a tight-lipped stare.

"I don't think she approves," Derek whispered. The encounter made him feel like a teenage boy.

"I think you're right." Kendal opened the gate. "I'll talk to her later. Mrs. Harris is my landlord and a good friend." Kendal adjusted her fedora in the car mirror. "She watches out for me."

"I need a hat." Derek said. "Can we stop at a store on the way?"

"Sure, I know a great place." She put the car in gear. "I shop there all the time."

Kendal parked in front of the surf shop. A tattoo parlor sat a couple of doors down. Derek made a mental note.

It was still early, and the surf shop was empty of customers. It appeared they had just opened. The young man working the counter couldn't take his eyes off Derek.

"The hats are over here." Kendal pointed.

"Why don't you pick one out for me?" he suggested. "You're the hat expert. I just need to cover my head so it doesn't burn."

"Hmm," she said. "I know you have conservative taste in clothes." She reached over to the rack and grabbed a dapper flat cap. "Try this one on." She stepped back to survey the look. "No, not quite." She grabbed a faded red baseball cap. "Here."

Derek hesitated. It reminded him of the one his dad had given him right before he died. The one he'd been wearing the day of the attack. But he knew he needed to move on—put the past behind him. He tugged the baseball cap on. She grinned.

"I believe that's the one. Go look in the mirror."

Just the word "mirror" made him inwardly cringe. Derek glanced at his reflection. "It's fine," he muttered, pulling out his credit card as he walked to the counter.

The young man took the card. "You're a doctor? You don't look like a doctor."

"Yeah, I'm a doctor," he agreed wearily. "And no, I don't look like a doctor."

"Do you have some form of identification?"

"Yes, I have my driver's license . . ." He realized how different the picture looked. "Never mind." He turned to Kendal. "I'm sorry but can you pay for this?"

"Sure." Kendal stepped up and pulled some bills from her wallet.

The kid rang it up and gave her the change.

"Nothing is ever easy," Derek muttered as they walked out of the store.

She laughed. "That's for sure."

Chapter 7

Kendal parked in the visitor section of the faculty parking lot, hoping to shorten their walk to the professor's office and avoid unwanted attention on the campus. In the main quad, she found a group of students who gave her directions to Dr. Jacob's office.

Derek felt like a circus sideshow.

"My back-up career," he said loudly to a group of students who stared and whispered as they walked by.

He had read on the internet that many of the old-time tattoo artists made most of their money by traveling with circuses during spring and summer, returning to their tattoo shops for the winter. The circus would showcase the tattoo artist's works where they would attract the paying customers. The posters and photos used for publicity were the only surviving records.

Daydreaming, he imagined himself in a man-thong on a poster, flexing muscles like a bodybuilder. *Step Right Up and See the TATMAN! The Amazing Illustrated Man, Tattooed from Head to Toe!*

He gave a mirthless chuckle. The article had gone on to explain that the connection between tattooing and the circus began in 1804 when Jean Baptiste Capri, who had been tattooed by the Marquesas, became a carnival performer. It said that in Capri's final years, he was forced to compete with trained dogs and other popular amusements in country fairs. By 1822, he had died, poor and forgotten.

Looking around at the judgmental stares, Derek had the overwhelming feeling that his future might not be much brighter.

He followed Kendal along the winding footpaths. Once inside the building, a young woman pointed them down the hall. The doors had name plates. When they reached Dr. Jacob's office, they found the old professor, pen in hand, seated at his desk. It was heaped with books and papers piled in stacks to be graded. He wore a blue button-up shirt with the sleeves rolled up. The professor looked a bit wrinkled, his red tie hanging loose.

"Hello, Dr. Jacob. I'm Kendal Reed. I spoke to you earlier." Kendal extended her hand. "Professor Andrews sends his regards."

"I wasn't expecting you so soon." He smiled. "Ah, Jake Andrews. He and I go way back. I haven't seen him for years. So, what can I do for—" Dr. Jacob stopped midsentence when Kendal stepped aside to introduce Derek. The professor's bushy eyebrows lifted over his glasses.

"I know one of your programs teaches ethnomusicology," she said. "From my understanding, that means that you study the social and cultural aspects of music. You also teach anthropology classes about South American Indians. As I explained on the phone, we may be interested in a specific tribe. The woman spoke Spanish and had tattoos on her face and arm." She paused. "I know it sounds totally crazy, but I think she may have put some type of hex on Dr. Hollinger."

The professor looked startled. "Can you tell me what happened?

"I'm not sure," Derek said, holding Dr. Jacob's gaze and keeping his voice calm. The professor might be his only chance of getting to the bottom of this and he needed the man to trust him. To *believe* him. "A few days ago, I didn't have a single tattoo. They appeared literally overnight, while I was sleeping. But let me rewind . . . I had an altercation with this woman in front of a hotel. Afterwards, I was physically sick." He gazed down at his inked hands. "Then I woke up almost two days later looking like this."

Dr. Jacob frowned but gave them a nod. "Come in, sit, sit. I'll help you if I can. Let's start with what she looked like."

Derek stepped into the small office. "A small, brown-skinned woman. Her hair was shoulder-length and black with streaks of gray."

"Do you remember anything else?" Dr. Jacob asked.

"I think I remember just about everything. She was wearing a sarong-type dress. It had bright purples and blues, black . . . I remember there was some red, too. The dress came up high around her neck, like this."

Derek demonstrated by crisscrossing his arms across the front of his chest. "She had tattoos on her face and arms. A tattoo went along her forehead, outlining her face. It also circled her mouth and chin with lines coming down from her lips. Oh, and she spoke Spanish."

"How do you know she spoke Spanish?" Dr. Jacob asked.

"Because I speak a little myself. At least, it seemed to be a Latin-based language, and it sounded like Spanish."

The professor tapped his pen on the desk, thinking. "The Warao people are Spanish-speaking. You may have run across one of their shamans. The Warao's 10,000-year-old religion is quite complex." Dr. Jacob stood up from his desk. "Their cultural beliefs are derived from three major areas: Traditional narrative, cosmology, and shamanism. I believe I have a book here somewhere . . ." He slid a volume from the shelf. "Yes. Here it is. I think the area most relevant to this conversation would be shamanism."

Dr. Jacob carefully flipped the pages of the old leather-bound book. "They believe there are three major types of sickness cured by three different types of healers." Stopping to scan a page, he continued. "Here it is. *The Warao possess a well-developed ancestor cult. Spiritual beings that they believe occupy the edge of the world. One of them is called Nabarao, people from the river depths believed to be a mirror image of human life. They mate with the Warao women to engender monsters.*" His finger lingered on the page. "Hmm. They also believe in metamorphosis, which is the transforming of men into jaguars."

Sitting down, Dr. Jacob continued. "Spiritual beings, together with their principal wives, occupy the edge of the Warao world. Their spirits may be beneficial or malevolent and are mediated by the shaman. They believe that they are descended from an adventurous, heavenly figure, the primordial hunter."

Derek closed his eyes, trying to rein in his frustration. This information seemed useless. "What does a shaman do?"

Dr. Jacob flipped the pages. "A shaman is a person who communicates with the supernatural for purposes of maintaining order in the universe. This includes mortal and immortal worlds. The shaman will usually do this by singing or chanting."

"Okay! Now we're getting somewhere." Derek leaned forward in his seat.

"The most powerful tool of the Warao Shaman is a huge rattle called a Lebu Mataro," Dr. Jacob said.

"That's her! She held something just like that. I bet she's a shaman."

Dr. Jacob glanced up from the book. "There are many American Indian tribes that have used tattoos to represent their tribal history. The tattoos demonstrate their cultural status. They also have different symbols to represent important events. For example, they'll pick an animal that they have great respect for to represent their spiritual power.

"The Waraos sing lullabies describing dangerous animals and spirits in the rainforest to their children to educate and pass on their culture. They prepare their children for the supernatural part of their world and its dangers." He looked up from the book, peering at Derek over the top of his lenses. "What happened for her to want to curse you?"

Derek shifted in his chair. "It was an accident. I was having a panic attack. The old woman grabbed my arm, I pushed her away, and she fell, I think."

Dr. Jacob pushed his reading glasses back up on his nose. "The Waraos are renowned sorcerers and will not allow themselves to be mistreated. The dark side of the shaman's power is that they can inflict harm through their sorcery. They live on a different spiritual plane than we do. They can manifest dreams and form their beliefs through shamanic sessions. We have no clue as to the power they can unleash. I'm not surprised that the old woman manifested a curse after your physical altercation."

"It's still hard for me to believe," Derek muttered.

The professor cocked a brow. "Then what are you doing in my office asking questions about shamans? One minute you say she put a curse on you. The next you say you don't believe in that stuff. Which is it? It's obvious your conscious mind doesn't believe, but what about your subconscious? You said you understand Spanish, right?"

Derek lifted his shoulder in a half shrug. "Yeah. A little bit."

Dr. Jacob removed the tobacco pipe that sat on his desk from its holder. He leaned back in his chair to study it thoughtfully as he spoke. "That could help explain how your subconscious heard the words even though your conscious mind didn't. Our subconscious is running our life and following the instructions we give it through suggestion. Remember, the shaman acts as an intermediary between our world and the spirit world."

"So . . . you do think she somehow had the power to do this to me?"

"I'm not saying that she did this to you, but she can produce the words that have the power to affect a certain outcome. Your subconscious mind will accept something as true and may bring it to pass as a condition."

Derek glanced over at Kendal, who seemed mesmerized by what the doctor was saying.

Dr. Jacob leaned forward, set the pipe back in its holder, and clasped his hands together on top of the desk. "Let me explain . . . For example, at work you have a boss, and you have the employees."

"Right," Derek and Kendal answered in unison, then exchanged a quick smile.

"The duties and authority of each are predefined. Occasionally, the boss may step over the line and ask or even demand something out of the realm of the duties of an employee. The employee knows that they had better comply with the request because there may be some type of consequence or reprisal if they refuse, such as less desirable work conditions or passing them up for a promotion. At worst letting them go." Dr. Jacob was now in teaching mode. "Are you with me so far?"

Derek looked over at Kendal, then hesitantly answered. "Yes."

"The shaman is the village boss. In this way the shaman controls the people. They are in fear of what the shaman will do if they don't comply. That gives the shaman a lot of power."

"But I didn't even know she was a shaman," Derek protested.

"In your case, I believe that your subconscious reacted to the threat. She had the painting on her face. It probably had something to do with a ritual she was taking part in. Maybe seeing this illustration on her face affected you. This could have something to do with autosuggestion or even PTSD."

Derek stiffened. "Why would you think I have post-traumatic stress disorder?"

"I'm not saying *you* have PTSD. It's just something to consider. Many people go through traumatic events in their life, causing things like increased anxiety."

Derek glanced down at his hands. The anatomy of his bones was inked in black. "Yes. I had just had a run-in with some teenagers that had upset me."

"A disturbing event can cause flashbacks or trouble sleeping."

Derek rubbed the tops of his legs. "I haven't slept well," he admitted.

"Sometimes you may even see things that aren't really there," Dr. Jacob persisted.

Derek grabbed the arms of his chair. "Are you telling me that these tattoos are a figment of my imagination?"

Dr. Jacob shook his head. "No, no . . . But when symptoms become severe, a person may be ready to see a doctor about it. Even though the doctors aren't sure why some people get PTSD, they have treatments and drugs that may be able to alleviate some of the symptoms."

Derek adjusted his cap, nodding thoughtfully.

Dr. Jacob hesitated to let what he had just said sink in. Then he proceeded slowly. "There is also what is called somatoform disorder. In psychology, this type of mental disorder is characterized by physical symptoms that suggest physical illness or injury. These symptoms can't be explained by a general medical condition or the direct effect of a substance. It can be attributable to a panic disorder. These symptoms are the result of unexplained origins. The sufferers perceive their plight as real."

Derek slid forward in his chair. "Look at me. Wouldn't you say my plight is real? How do I get rid of these things?"

Dr. Jacob drummed his fingers on the desk. "There are religious devices, medals, artifacts . . . mixtures of herbs put in a pouch to hang around the neck. Some people think that carrying garlic or ginger will ward off a curse."

Derek shrank back. "What happens once you're already cursed. How do you reverse it?"

"Well, I'm sure there are reverse spells out there. I've heard it said that 'curses are like promises; they can be broken.' But you may want to consult an expert." He reached for his empty pipe and put the stem in his mouth. "And I am no expert, Dr. Hollinger."

Chapter 8

It was afternoon by the time they left the college. Kendal wasn't sure how she could help. She made lemonade and opened a beer for Derek. They sat together at the patio table.

"Do you really think I did this to myself?" he asked, picking at the label on the bottle.

"I don't know what to think." Kendal felt conflicted about telling him how she felt about his behavior toward her in the office.

Derek clenched his jaw. "What does that mean?"

Kendal's stomach began to churn. "That means I think the subconscious is a powerful thing. Something we are still learning about. I think you should go in for some psychoanalysis and see what they have to say."

Derek let out a sigh. "I'm ready to talk to anyone who can shed some light on this."

Kendal stood. "I'll call the doctor that Dr. Jacob suggested you contact and see how quickly you can get in to see her."

Derek remained on the deck, deep in thought.

Kendal watched him through the window. She could sense his anxiety. Did she really want to be a part of this? She was starting to get in too deep. She had enough of her own problems. But she couldn't bring herself to turn her back on him.

She reluctantly made the call.

Stepping back out on the patio, she said, "Okay, you can see her first thing in the morning. She had a cancellation."

Derek leaned back in his chair. "You think this doctor will have any clue to what is going on?"

She noticed he didn't even think to thank her. "I don't know." She forced a smile. "But let's not worry about it now. You want to go out for a little bit? Let's go get a drink and something to eat."

"Okay, but let's try to find someplace quiet. The fewer people we come in contact with, the better off I am right now."

"I know." She closed the slider behind them. "I already have a place in mind."

He grinned. "I bet you do."

"Now what is that supposed to mean?"

"Nothing. I'm just messing around." He frowned. "Don't be so sensitive."

"Really? Are you really saying that to *me* right now? You think *I'm sensitive*? After all the crap you've thrown at me in the past year?"

"What are you talking about?"

"Never mind." Her face shut down. "Forget it."

"No." He reached out for her. "I really want to know."

Kendal closed her eyes for a moment, inhaling the masculine scent of his body as she tried to calm herself.

"Look at me."

She stared at his chest, focusing on the black swirls connecting the tattoos. He gently lifted her chin. She had tears in her eyes. Derek looked surprised—and guilty.

"What did I do to upset you like this?'

"Are you kidding me? What haven't you done?" Kendal pulled away.

"No. I really don't know why you are so upset. Tell me what I've done." His voice softened. "Please."

She threw her purse down, went over to the refrigerator, and grabbed a beer. Then she went out to the patio. Derek quickly grabbed his own beer and followed. He sat in silence, waiting for her to start.

Kendal took a deep breath. "When I first came here, I was a different person."

"Yes. You were."

She hung her head. "Until I came to California, I really didn't know who I was. I had been living an unhealthy existence. I dreamed of starting a new life." She raised her chin, savoring the cool ocean air. "And *I did that all by myself.*"

Exhaling deeply, she continued. "I had a lot of things to work through from my childhood. Mostly abandonment issues." She watched the trees sway in the breeze. "I never had anyone that I could turn to or depend on while growing up. I lived in a predatory environment. I promised myself that I would never be put in that situation again." She turned her gaze back to Derek. "I also promised myself that I would create a happy, successful life."

"Well, it seems you've done a good job."

"Really?" She eyed him. "Then why have you been so hard on me?"

"Hard on you?" He cocked his head. "When was I hard on you?"

"Every time I've made a step forward, like reorganizing the clinic or decorating your office . . ." She jutted out her lip. "You never had anything encouraging to say."

Derek sat back and crossed his arms. "I didn't realize—"

"Oh, come on! You weren't just negative. You can be downright cruel."

"Now wait a second!" Derek pursed his lips. "How can you say that? I've always rewarded you with a raise every time you straightened something out in the office."

"That's not what I'm talking about." She sat back in her chair. "Yes, you have given me money. Tell you the truth, that's the only thing that has kept me around."

"Ouch. That hurts." He winced.

She looked down at her hands. "Every time you gave me grief on my appearance, it stung."

"I looked at it as teasing."

"No, you didn't. You said some pretty cruel things." Her eyes started welling up. "When I colored my hair red, you made so many rude comments that you made me cry at least once a day."

He looked up at her, appalled. "Cry?" he whispered.

She wiped the tears away. "So many times I lost count. When I pierced my nose, you made comments to the patients. I could see even they felt uncomfortable for me."

His shoulders slumped. "I didn't realize I was that bad."

"And what about the tattoo I have on my ankle?" She put her leg out. "What did you say about that?"

He looked at the sun tattooed on her ankle. "I don't remember."

"You said it was a white trash thing to do."

Derek looked up and chuckled. "Well, I guess I'm ready to be tossed in the trash heap then."

"Yes, you are." Kendal let out a small laugh.

"I'm sorry. I've been a real jerk." He looked at her with pleading eyes and reached out a hand. She let him take hers, but let it lie limp.

"Well, just think about this," she said. "Look at the changes you're going through right now. What if I had treated you with the same contempt?"

"I have no idea where I would be right now." He squeezed her hand. "You're the only reason I've been able to deal with this as well as I have."

"Well, think about what *I've* been through. I grew up in a dysfunctional, abusive household, with no emotional support." She took her hand back. "This has been my chance to build a whole new life."

She got up from her chair and walked over to the rail. "The people now closest to me have had a major influence. You being one. I've been able to grow into my career and become very independent financially." She turned back toward him. "But those hurtful comments hit me hard."

"I guess when I saw you changing . . ." He rubbed his head. "I think I was afraid that if you changed too much, you were going to leave."

"Well, the way you've been treating me—"

He walked over to face her. "I've handled it all wrong."

She lifted her chin. "Yes, you definitely have."

"I'm sorry." He reached for her hands. "Can you forgive me?

The last thing I want to happen is for you to leave."

She started to pull away. "Of course, you say that *now*."

Derek held her hands tighter. "No, really. I'm telling you, that's why I think my behavior is so bad. I act out because I only think about me. What *I'm* feeling . . . I didn't like the change. The more you modified your look, the less it seemed that you needed me."

"Is that what you think?" She pulled her hands back. "That I'm dependent on you?"

He shook his head. "No, not in that way. I mean the more stable and successful, the more confident Kendal . . . I just felt it was a matter of time before you would be out looking for someone . . . something else. You know, a job change."

She leaned back on the rail. "Well, except for you giving me a hard time, I feel like I have just the right amount of responsibility. I know the three doctors I work with will keep me busy and growing. I have free rein to run the office as I like."

"You really are good at what you do." He leaned on the rail beside her. " I've grown dependent on you. I don't want you to leave. Not just because of this situation, which I will never be able to repay you for . . ."

"I don't expect you to repay me. This is what friends do for each other."

He turned toward her. "Does this mean we're friends?"

She smiled slightly. "Only if you don't say mean things to me anymore."

"Is it all right if I tell you *why* I'm having the anxiety, instead of making snide comments? Will that work?" Derek grabbed both the beers off the table. He handed Kendal her bottle.

She let out a sigh. "Yes, I think that'll work." She raised her bottle.

He clicked his bottle with hers, then took a sip. "You hungry?"

"I am." She took the last sip and threw the bottle in the trash.

A few minutes later, Kendal and Derek stood looking up at the menu of a hot dog stand located around the corner from her apartment.

"I've never eaten at a place like this before," Derek admitted.

"Seriously?" She eyed him with amusement. "Do you like hot dogs? They have Polish sausage, too."

"Yeah, I do." He grinned at her. "I've just never gone out to dinner to specifically eat one."

Kendal gave him a sideways look. "Wow."

Derek put his hands in his back pockets. "What can I tell you? I've had a pretty sheltered life, mostly by design."

Their hot dogs were ready immediately. They sat at one of the picnic tables out front.

"I know your teenage years were pretty bad," she said. "Recovering from your injuries. Having to catch up with your schooling. But what about college? You must have had a better time in college?"

"I really didn't get involved with anyone," Derek confessed. He took a bite of the hot dog and wiped the mustard from the corner of his mouth. "Dr. Casey was still alive. He was my mentor. He took care of me through my injuries, reconstructed my face. He was the reason I was able to catch up with my studies, then go to college. He paid for everything. He was like a father to me. While I was going through college, I worked with him."

He gave a short laugh. "I pretty much have spent my entire life preparing for my career. He was driven and I was driven. We both loved what we were doing and shared it with each other. I was pretty focused."

"Well, that explains a lot."

"Why?"

"You seem much older than your age. You know, really serious about everything. But then when it comes to the simple things like going out for a hot dog . . ." She shrugged. "You've never experienced it before."

"After Dr. Casey died, I just continued to focus on the practice. I took partners on because I knew I couldn't handle the patient load by myself." He eyed her seriously. "When you came in, you were a godsend, Kendal. I needed someone who had both business sense and medical experience."

"Have you ever dated?" She tucked her hair behind one ear.

"I did a little bit in college. I never took a serious interest in anyone."

"What about since you've owned the business?"

"I dated a couple of women." His eyes twinkled.

"You have never had anyone special? Ever?" She fiddled with her earring.

"No one special. What about you? Have you dated since you came to California?" He crunched up the dirty napkin, looking around for a place to throw it.

"I find that the men here are pretty selfish and immature."

His shoulders slumped. "Is that directed toward me?"

"If the shoe fits," she joked. "No, Derek. The guys I've met just seem to be more into themselves than they are into having a serious relationship."

"I see." He played with the hot dog paper in his hand.

"Do you think you'll ever get married?" Kendal asked.

He sat up straight, gaze distant. "I hope so."

"How are you going to do that if you stay married to your business?" she teased.

"I guess that's something I'm going to have to consider." He rubbed his chin. "If I can find a way out of this mess. But I don't think I'll be such a great catch if I lose my business and end up in a circus sideshow."

She touched his arm. "Come on . . . don't think that way. You must stay positive."

Derek stared into space. "When I start to think about the reality of what my future might be, it can be pretty depressing."

"That's why you have to focus on each day and what you need to do to have a better tomorrow."

He cocked his head sideways. "Wow, I like that. You should write song lyrics."

She crumpled her own napkin and started to clean the table. "That's the way I've had to think. If I didn't take control and decide what was going to happen next, there is no way I would be living the kind of life I am here."

Kendal sipped the last of her drink. She reached out and took the hot dog paper from his hands, throwing their trash into the bin. The parking lot was now empty, and the hot dog stand had closed.

"Hey, what do you say we go release my motorcycle from its captors?" Derek asked in a more cheerful tone. "I think this would be a good time to go get it."

The sight of his smile gave her a little flutter. "That sounds like a good idea."

Kendal and Derek guest parked in front of his penthouse building.

"Go inside and tell the security guard that we're here to pick up the motorcycle for Dr. Hollinger to have it serviced tomorrow," he suggested. "They'll check for your name on the list. Then we'll drive down to the garage to get my bike."

Derek waited as Kendal entered the lobby. Within a few minutes she was back.

"No problem. They didn't even ask me for my ID."

He shook his head ruefully. "That really upsets me that this is so easy."

"Why? Don't you want it to be easy?"

"For me, yes." He cocked a brow. "But what if it wasn't me? This would be a pretty simple scam don't you think?"

"Yeah, I guess you're right."

She started the engine then turned into the underground parking garage.

"Turn left," he directed her. "Keep going . . . it's the next turn."

She rounded the corner. "My pride and joy," he joked, eyeing the Harley. "Right next to the love of my life." Derek's gaze briefly rested on the Bentley parked in the next space. He winked and Kendal rolled her eyes.

"You can go down to the end to turn around while I get my helmet out of the cabinet."

Kendal followed his instructions. When she pulled up, Derek stood smiling with two helmets in his hand. He was still wearing his faded red baseball cap and a brown leather jacket. He hefted one of the helmets. "Got one for you."

She took it from his hand. "We'll see about that. I want to see you ride that thing first."

Kendal watched as he took his cap off and tossed it onto the front seat of her car. He put the helmet on, then walked the motorcycle backwards. He twisted the key and hit the starter button. The engine roared to life, echoing through the underground garage.

He gave her a little salute. "See you at home." Derek dropped the visor and put the bike in gear. The bike eased forward and turned in front of Kendal's car, then sped off.

Kendal felt that tingling feeling in her stomach as she followed closely behind.

Once back at the apartment, Derek sat down on the couch. Kendal had a strong desire to sit down next to him. She was beginning to feel tempted to give in to the attraction. Then the constraints of better judgment kicked in. *Don't be led astray*, she thought.

"Good night, Derek, sweet dreams." She reluctantly closed her bedroom door.

Stay on course, her inner voice chided as she got ready for bed. *He's a mess. It might be gratifying in the short term, but what if he breaks your heart?*

❧❧❧

Derek lay on the couch, hands laced behind his head. Kendal continued to surprise him. She was beautiful, smart, strong, and

(88)

compassionate—not to mention forgiving, since she'd put up with his selfish behavior without quitting. He resolved to treat her as she deserved from now on. Getting to know Kendal Reed was the only silver lining of the whole situation.

As he started to unwind, his thoughts wandered to the things the UCLA professor had said. He was anxious to talk to the psychologist in the morning. Maybe she would have some answers.

His eyes slid shut . . .

He was back at school, walking toward the big double doors. A dense, sticky web stretched between them, blocking his path. His heart began to pound.

Where was the spider? He spun around, the hair on the back of his neck prickling with the certainty that he was being stalked. He could see through the sticky silk strands to the sidewalk.

In the middle of the web danced three demons dressed as men. They wore no shoes and had taloned feet. Waving clawed hands in the air, one brandished a stick. Derek instinctively knew that their circular movement inspired evil and terror through supernatural attacks.

He woke in a cold sweat, then sat up on the couch to stare into the darkness. He pictured himself walking down the sidewalk that fateful day. The agony of the attack was still fresh in his mind. The unthinkable had happened. Thugs had stolen his childhood innocence. His life shattered, never to be the same. Why hadn't he just run?

Forgiveness was not in the cards. Twenty-five years later, what lesson was life trying to teach him?

"How is this all connected?" he muttered angrily. "Why do they still haunt me?"

Derek dozed off again. He sat straight up on the couch, ready to fight, drifting in and out of demon-filled dreams.

Chapter 9

Derek decided to leave the apartment at the same time Kendal left for work. He didn't want to be left alone with his dark thoughts.

For anonymity, he put his helmet on before he left the apartment in broad daylight. They walked together to the street. Kendal smiled and waved as he watched her pull out.

Derek sat paralyzed on his bike. The apprehension of today's evaluation had conjured up every possible thing that could go wrong. He knew that the fear of a negative evaluation was the hallmark of social anxiety. But knowing this information didn't help. Nothing had changed the fact that he felt like an alien.

He looked at the address Kendal had put on his phone. The one-story office building sat in a strip mall just two miles away. He summoned the courage to zip up his leather jacket over his hoody, put on his gloves, then start his bike. Luckily, he didn't have far to go. He slowly released the clutch until he felt the bike pull away.

When he reached the strip mall parking lot, he parked his bike. He took his helmet off and quickly put on his baseball cap and raised his hood.

Behind the sign on the door that read *Dr. Margaret Cole Ph.D., MFT, Life Coach* sat a simple wooden desk. Worn cushioned chairs bookended a sickly-looking palm. Two miniature stools and a battered bookcase filled with children's books flanked a fish tank bubbling loudly.

A tall, striking woman with short-cropped gray hair appeared from one of the doorways. She was reading some papers in a folder and looked up with light green eyes.

"Hello." She flashed pearly white teeth.

"I have an appointment with Dr. Cole," he replied.

"You must be Dr. Hollinger." She set the folder on the desk and held out her hand. "I'm Dr. Cole, it's nice to meet you."

She didn't seem surprised by the number of tattoos. He felt grateful that Kendal must have already warned the doctor about his appearance when she made the appointment.

"Call me Derek." He gave a wry grin. "I don't feel much like a doctor these days."

"Okay, Derek, come on back."

He followed her down a short hall.

"This is my office. Sorry about the mess. My assistant has been out sick for a couple of days. I've been on my own." She walked around the desk that took up most of the space and sat down in front of a window, then motioned toward the chair in front of her desk.

Derek sat down and waited.

She took the files that were on the desk and stacked them on the floor. "So, what brings you to see me today?"

He pulled down the hood and took off his cap. "You're looking at it."

Dr. Cole regarded him calmly. "Explain what you mean."

"The tattoos." He held out both hands, turning his palms up, then back, rotating his arms back and forth, showing the tattoos on both sides. "You can't see the walking billboard here?"

"These tattoos upset you?"

"Hell, yes, they upset me." He ran his hand over his skull. "I just woke up Monday morning and they were there."

"How do you suppose they could have gotten there?"

"That's why I'm here to see you!" Derek drew a deep breath, trying to stay calm. "I am trying to figure that out, doctor."

She leaned forward. "You must have some clue?"

"I have a couple of hunches." He played with his cap.

"Start there," she suggested softly.

"Do you want me to start with what happened this last weekend, or why I think I have these on me now?" He hunched in his chair, feeling the weight of the world on his shoulders.

"I think it would be best for you to start at the beginning so I can put all the pieces together."

Derek walked her through his childhood. The story took almost an hour to tell. She finished writing the last of her notes and laid her pen down. "I must admit, it's a unique situation. I've never run across anything remotely like this before."

He nodded impatiently. "But you believe me? About all of it?"

"I do. And your assistant confirmed the sudden onset of these tattoos."

He sighed with relief.

"My first thought is you should be aware that your anxiety from these tattoos on your skin could be fueled by destructive thoughts. These thoughts are charged with fear that may be lodged in your subconscious mind. I believe that if you can succeed at cleansing or replacing these thoughts, you could possibly experience a healing or a change in your condition. Your attitude can bring about a harmonious union of the conscious and the subconscious mind which in turn releases the healing power."

Derek's attention was locked on her. The doctor paused, then looked down at her notes.

"It sounds like the shaman woman who you say put the curse on you may have activated all your greatest fears, worries and anxiety created by past physical injuries, in turn unleashing the post-traumatic stress that you have been suppressing since childhood. Her incantation touched your subconscious mind to make you think that she produced the results that you see on your body."

Derek tensed at the realization that they might be on the right track with the shaman woman.

Stroking her chin with her index finger, she continued. "I believe this tapestry on your skin could represent a lifetime of hurt and despair. Let me clarify how this type of control in your subconscious mind works. It can be provoked by the suggestions of another."

"Are you referring to when the shaman woman started chanting at me?" Derek asked.

"Yes. Your subconscious mind can be controlled by suggestion and/or by implementation. In your case one and the other were used with the chanting and the noise of the rattle. The reaction is purely subjective; everyone has different responses. Some people will react, others will be unfazed. In your case, you were a powder keg waiting for the match to be lit."

Dr. Cole regarded him thoughtfully. "I'm sure at the time you thought of it as being the ranting of an old woman. You had no idea the impact it would have on you physically. But let me be clear. I am not saying she did this to you. I am exploring the facts as you have presented them to me. My job is to treat you for your psychological welfare."

Derek shifted in his seat. "Fair enough."

"This in turn caused your subconscious to absorb the invocation, immediately influencing the autonomic nervous system, which generated the markings on your skin. It seemed that at the time of the event, you were in no frame of mind to make any independent judgment as to what was happening."

What could the old woman's intention have been? He wondered.

Dr. Cole flicked at a bit of dust on the corner of her desk. "You slept through the next thirty-two hours. You abandoned your willpower and the autosuggestion was able to succeed."

"If this turns out to be the case, then what can I do to reverse it?" Derek asked.

She raised her eyebrows and pursed her lips. "The kinetic action of the subconscious mind continues throughout sleep. You may experience more illumination."

"Oh, my God!" He grabbed his head. "Please don't tell me this is going to keep happening."

"No, that's not what I'm saying. But you *can* take back control. Much of the power to change this revolves around the trigger for this reaction and the stories you tell yourself going forward. Remember, the events of the past are what lead you to form the beliefs and assumptions that guide the future."

She relaxed and folded her hands together on top of her desk. "You see, most people believe that their beliefs are unchangeable truths. They are unaware that they have authored their own stories. Just the way you told me your story is how you habitually talk about your life. You should examine your role and challenge the story. Then maybe you can start to rewrite the story of your life as a more positive experience. Whether you do it out loud or silently on paper, it will be constructive in shaping your current circumstances."

She crossed her ankles to one side of her chair and leaned forward with her hands still folded. "Think of the areas that you have been successful in your life. Could this be in direct relation to your life experiences? Think of the skills you have acquired. Would you have taken the same road if you had not had that life experience? Do you understand where I am going with this?"

Derek nodded. "Yes, I think I do."

"The idea is to rewrite your story to a new positive." She picked up a notebook, opened it to a blank page, and pointed to it. "Start over. Write the story on a clean slate. Once rewritten, you can start to live your new positive life by retelling your new story every day. Your thoughts and actions will generate the momentum necessary to truly believe what it is you are saying. Make sure you tell someone else, someone you can trust, who believes in you. Remember that you are the author of your life. Only you can determine whether it is a good life or a bad life according to your perception."

Again, he nodded. "I'm following, doctor."

"One of the things you can do to get the process started is to take the time right before you drop off to sleep to reinforce the blessing associated with being talented and successful. You are obviously accomplished and smart. What events had to take place for these positive outcomes to happen to you in your life? These events may not all be positive but by using lemons to make lemonade . . . you understand the concept."

Derek's mind immediately flashed back to the beating. He forced himself to focus as Dr. Cole pushed up with both hands to stand.

"I think right there is a very good foundation in which to start," she said encouragingly. "Thoughts of harmony and perfect health with clear skin. Imagine your clear, perfect skin on your body as you slip off to sleep."

"I'll try," he said, covering his skepticism.

Leaning in with her hands on the desk, Dr. Cole continued. "I strongly suggest you cease talking about your tattoos in a negative way. Associate them with everything positive. Upsetting thoughts and emotional distress can reflect an imbalance in your neurotransmitters. These are the chemical messengers that calm or stimulate your brain cells."

He nodded tersely. "I'm aware of that. I *did* go to medical school."

"Of course." She smiled. "I suggest you give the tattoos names which draw your attention to the positive. You must become a mental surgeon. Cut off these negative thoughts like you would any other cancer or unwanted growth." She slashed the air with her pen. "By giving these tattoos negative attention, the kinetic action is inhibited, which in turn diminishes the release of the healing power and energy in your subconscious mind. Start to walk forward and step out of the past."

Derek sighed. "How do I step forward when I have the past written all over me?"

"You have experienced the gratitude of your patients. This has affected your subconscious." Her eyes darted to a thank-you card sitting on a shelf. "Plug into that. Use the positives. Use every little positive that happens in your day to your advantage."

Kendal's smile flashed into Derek's mind.

"When you find that you are starting to think or talk negatively, reverse it. Make sure you busy your mind with concepts of harmony, health, and good will. The professional treatment of your patients is a perfect example of a conscious movement of thought. When something on your patient's body has been reconstructed, they feel better. Correct?"

She used the pen in her hand as a pointer, cocking her head. "You do think about the work and how it affects your patients, right?"

Derek sat straight up. "Sure, I do."

"Use the positive feeling that you receive when you heal a patient . . . Use that positive feeling to rework your subconscious." She made a circle in the air with her pen. "Absorb it. In turn these tattoos should start to dissolve. Try to take the time to be still."

She closed her eyes. "Quiet your mind. Focus on your breath." She placed one hand on her stomach. "Let your abdomen expand as you inhale deeply while counting to ten."

Derek mimicked her, closing his eyes and drawing a long, slow breath.

"Hold your breath for two counts and then breathe out to a count of seven. Tell yourself that you know that the deeper wisdom of your subconscious is responding. Tell yourself that you have the right to be happy, healthy, and successful. Your subconscious will respond. Repeat this throughout the day, especially during calm moments. By doing this, your brain and body will start to relearn the new story you are telling it. You will be creating the right frame of mind. This is a good start for you."

Derek opened his eyes, feeling refreshed, energized.

"Just concentrate on this for now," Dr. Cole suggested. "Let's talk again tomorrow."

Derek slowly stood and extended his tattooed hand. "Thank you, Doctor. This gives me a lot to think about."

She took his hand firmly. "Remember, believe in perfect health, happiness, peace, and above all, divine guidance. The forces of nature are not evil. Man creates his own thoughts, which manifest his own destiny and misery. So, if someone criticizes you for the way you look, rejoice, give thanks, and appreciate the opportunity that you are getting to start a new life. Take it as a reminder of where you are going, not where you have been. Use it to your advantage." She smiled. "I'll text you for the time of your next appointment."

Derek gave a nod as he put his baseball cap back on. He did not put the hoodie back up when he walked out of the office door. Mounting the bike, he took the cap off and put his helmet on. The hum of the engine vibrated his helmet as he thought about the times he had given Kendal grief about a new hair color, her clothes, or her tattoo. Guilt gnawed at him. How could he have been so judgmental?

Being a man of science, he knew that we all live in a world of laws. But he had never taken the time to nurture his spiritual life. Instead, he had devised a blueprint of fear, worry, anxiety, and stress. He had woven a perfect negative pattern into his subconscious. It had become a complex web of such a grotesque magnitude that it had now manifested in the form of physical tattoos. He was starting to realize that he had built the perfect emotional wall to keep people out—until it collapsed and buried him in the rubble.

What have I done to myself? he thought, releasing the clutch as the bike lurched forward.

Chapter 10

After leaving the doctor's office, Derek took a long ride to mull over what had transpired in the session and to digest the information. One thing had become clear: his violent history had probably created this overwhelming feeling of distress, fear, and helplessness. The traumatic childhood event also seemed to have changed how his body responded to emotions, memory, and the way he thought.

When stressful events occurred, it triggered his body to feel like it was reliving the attack. He didn't realize until the tattoos had materialized how isolated and out of control his behavior had become. Now maybe he could start recognizing the related triggers caused by the violent attack. He also now understood that his trouble sleeping, anxiety, and fear of personal relationships were symptoms of his trauma.

But as pressing as his own problems were, Derek understood that Kendal had also experienced the trauma of ongoing abuse in her childhood. At the office, he'd wrongly believed she was a rebel looking for negative attention. Now he grasped that she had made great efforts to escape her childhood story, to create her new and improved adult one—and that *he* had been a stumbling block in her progress.

It was time for him to face the unpleasant truth head-on. No more lying to himself. No more hiding behind the trappings of money and success.

Derek decided to ride over to the tattoo parlor he had seen the previous morning when he and Kendal had stopped to buy his baseball cap. Upon arrival, he sat on his bike outside Tremendous Tattoos, reading the advertisements on the window.

OPEN DAILY: NOON to 10 PM

Walk-Ins Welcome

Tattooing Only

Derek checked his watch. He got off his bike and put his helmet on the seat. Pulled his cap out of his jacket and put it on his head, then opened the front door of the tattoo shop, triggering the buzzer.

Low-hanging lights illuminated the twelve-by-twelve-foot room. Along the walls were reclining-type chairs and small tables filled with colored inks and tattoo guns. Pictures advertised samples of the different types of tattoos offered.

Out from behind a strand of hanging beads appeared a goateed, heavily inked individual wiping his hands on a towel. "Hey, what's up man? What can I do for you?"

Derek gave a friendly smile. "I'm just here to see if I can get some information."

"Ah, well, I'll see what I can do. I'm not here all the time. The owner is out to lunch. I'm kind of watching the place, so it depends on what it is you're looking for."

"I just want information on the meaning of some of these tattoos I have."

"Really?" The man looked confused. "Looks like you got some

nice work. You must have thought they meant something when you had 'em done."

He gave a weak grin. "I was pretty drunk."

The man laughed. "Been there, brother. We have a book that might help." He pointed over to a small coffee table that sat in front of a couch. "Be my guest. You can look at it, just don't take it anywhere. Terry will have my head."

"Not a problem," Derek said quickly.

"Make yourself at home. I'm doing some designs for a friend. I need to get 'em done by tonight." He disappeared into the back again.

Derek sat down and opened a book on the history of tattooing.

For thousands of years tattooing has been as much of a statement of world views as it has been of the simple form of self-expression. Humans, nature, and the supernatural landscape united together creating an interlaced fabric that documents a range of ideas on the sacred geography of the skin, our most natural canvas.

"Yeah," he muttered dryly. "I'm a canvas, all right."

Tattooed images represent the close relationship between humans and the rest of nature. The supernatural forces were cajoled and appealed to, for the benefit of the indigenous people who sought to acquire access to their ancestors. These were more than just skin-deep symbols. Tapping into them would allow the body to escape into a world where there is the magical essence of things detached from the here and now.

He flipped the page.

Three hundred years ago, there may have been more tattooed tribes living in the dense jungles and swamps of South America than anywhere else in the world. Some groups tattooed for medicinal purposes and some to ward off evil spirits. Others etched designs into their bodies to show success in battle. Still others attempted to transform themselves into predatory animals or to gain spiritual guardians with their ritual markings.

Europeans introduced diseases to which the local people had no natural immunity. Epidemics like Hepatitis C and measles have claimed the lives of elders, shamans, and tattoo masters, each of whom were the gatekeepers of the traditions like tattooing and the known associations with them.

Derek skipped down the page. *Men who had partaken in perilous journeys or headhunting raids away from the security of the longhouse were true warriors and were also tattooed . . .*

After skimming the history book, Derek still had mixed feelings. He was well aware of the perception that he was probably trying to bring some fantasy to life. He knew when a person chose to wear tattoos head to toe it would solicit opinions that tend to be judgmental because they made the person look scary.

The display of tattoos on a person's body often were there to represent the person's deepest desires. An outer physical expression of their imagination. But to Derek it seemed to be a type of escapism. An overt way to telegraph one's beliefs to the world. It also seemed to be a form of a risk-taking behavior. Impulsive and thrill-seeking. Another way to stand out from the crowd.

He also instinctively knew that people had a different perception of him when he dressed in his doctor's coat than in a T-shirt and jeans, covered head to toe in tattoos. For Derek, the diametrical reality connected to his past self and his current uniqueness had been supplanted—his self-esteem stolen.

He stuck his head through the beads hanging in the doorway. "Hey, buddy, thanks."

A distracted wave. "Sure, you bet."

Outside the tattoo parlor, he put on his sunglasses. It took a second for his eyes to adjust. The little café across the street looked like a place he could get a burger. Once inside, Derek sat at a table and ordered from the waitress.

Picking up his glass of iced tea, he glanced across to a table where a patron sat reading a magazine.

The magazine slowly came down. A stern-faced man with military-style cropped gray hair cocked one of his bushy eyebrows. In a gravelly voice he asked, "Where'd you get inked?"

"Pardon?"

"Where'd you get your work done?"

"I didn't," Derek replied defiantly.

"What kind of answer is that?" the man barked.

"The truth," Derek replied.

"Then where did all that work come from?"

Derek shifted in his chair. "That's a hard question to answer."

A low rumbling noise came from his throat. "Well, now, you really got my interest." The stranger grabbed his coffee cup and sat down at Derek's table. "I'm Terry." It sounded like rocks rolling from his throat. "I own the tattoo shop across the street."

"Terry! I was just in your shop looking for you!" Derek grinned with relief.

"And now you've found me," Terry rasped.

"I wanted to ask you some questions about the tattoos."

"Okay. But you have to answer my question first."

"Sure, what question is that?" Derek sat straight up in his chair.

"Where did you get all that tattoo work done?" Terry persisted.

"Like I told you, I didn't have the work done." He looked around and lowered his voice. "I just woke up a couple of days ago and I was illustrated like this head to toe." Derek raised a hand. "Swear to God."

"Ha!" Terry laughed. "No way. Really, who did your work?"

"I'm serious." Derek was getting tired of the interrogation.

"You can't be."

"I am."

Terry leaned back. "There's no way that you can wake up and already have all this work done. This takes years to do."

"I know. That's what I thought and that's one of the reasons I want to talk to you." He sighed. "I know it sounds nuts, but I think a shaman woman put a curse on me and I manifested them, kind of like stigmata or something."

Derek held eye contact. Terry looked uncertain.

"That's the craziest thing I ever heard. You must be pulling my leg." He looked around the café. "Someone hired you to mess with me, right?"

Derek took out his wallet. "Here's my identification. I'm a doctor." He slid his driver's license across the table, then handed Terry a business card. "I can't even go back to work right now because I can't let anyone know this has happened. It would ruin my career."

Terry read the business card. "I still don't think I believe you." He picked up the driver's license, looking at the picture, then looking back at Derek.

"Call my office, ask for Kendal Reed. She's the head nurse and office manager. Tell her who you are and she'll confirm what I'm telling you."

Terry pulled out his cell phone and called the number on the card.

"Kendal, please," his voice boomed.

"May I ask who is calling?"

He had his phone volume loud enough that Derek could hear Nicole's voice faintly from across the table.

"Tell her a friend of Dr. Hollinger."

Terry put the cell phone on speaker. Her singsong voice rang out. "Hold, please."

The two men listened to the Muzak, staring at each other in silence while Terry waited for Kendal to come to the phone.

Finally, the hold music cut off. "Good afternoon, this is Kendal."

"Kendal, this is Terry. I own Tremendous Tattoos, the tattoo shop downtown."

"Oh, Terry." Her voice grew friendlier. "Derek said he might stop by your shop today. What can I do for you?"

"Is your Dr. Hollinger an illustrated man?"

"Yes, Terry, he is," Kendal whispered.

In a raspy voice, he asked, "And how did he become that illustrated man?"

"We don't know. That's why he's there to talk to you," she responded in a flat voice.

"Okay, thank you, Kendal."

"Thank you, Terry."

Terry hit the button on his cell phone and looked up at Derek. "Well, I'll be damned."

"Yep," Derek agreed.

He grunted. "I still don't know if I believe it or not."

"Join the club."

"So, what do you want from me?"

"Information."

"What kind of information?" he asked, pushing his phone back into his shirt pocket.

"First about the tattoos. What would you say if I told you a shaman woman gave me this full body of tattoos?"

"First, I would say you are full of it. But then I would say I have seen some weird and unbelievable things in my time. I served twenty-two years in the Marines in some remote places in the world. Strange things happen in far-off places. You could never imagine unless you had seen these things for yourself. We killed a twelve-foot giant in a cave in Afghanistan." He hesitated. "I can give you a little history from my experiences."

The waitress came to the table. "I would appreciate that," Derek said as he watched her set a plate of food down in front of him, then refill his iced tea glass.

"Shamans use tattoos for magical and medicinal purposes. They believe they have the help of the spirits. They chant to ward off evil spirits. I served in Indonesia for a while. The tattooed individuals I saw believed that their tattoos kept their souls close. Women in some regions of the world wear the tattoos on their face to appease the spirits of the afterlife. Some tattoos are believed to lure game animals into their villages.

"I know the Philippine shamans would work their medicine to cure their patients of soul loss, which they attributed to disease. The spirits they summoned could be from human or animal. The treatment might require an application of medicinal tattoos on a particular part of the body." Terry frowned. "Hey, maybe that's what's going on with you. Maybe you were tattooed to hide you from the evil spirits that are after you."

Derek took a bite of his burger and chewed thoughtfully. "Maybe. I can't rule anything out at this point."

"The people I saw in remote regions that were tattooed mostly practiced shamanism. It's the oldest spiritual religion, been around since the dawn of time. Mythology was developed out of these rituals. It was a way to relieve the guilt of the hunt, whether it was human or animal. That way they felt they could keep a balance between the spirits and the dead."

Terry folded his arms, resting a thumb on his chin. "We heard some crazy stories from the guys who served in Vietnam. They said they saw gruesome animal sacrifices in the jungle that represented offerings to satisfy the spirits. That's why when you see a heavily tattooed indigenous person, the tattoos are there to provoke fear. This has been going on since the dawn of man."

Derek wiped his mouth. "I never thought about the history of tattoos and how far they go back in time. I only knew that tattooing wasn't something I would ever be interested in. I never had a reason to think about it—except for the obvious reason of not wanting to mess up a perfectly good body."

"I look at it as improving on perfection," Terry bantered.

"I have a different thought as how to improve on perfection, obviously, as a plastic surgeon."

"You improve on perfection only if you are an artist, and I believe that inking is an art."

Plastic surgery is the truest form of the art, Derek thought, though he didn't say it out loud.

"Now when I was stationed in Japan," Terry continued, "I learned a lot about tattoos. There was a law made by the royalty and elite that said ornate kimonos couldn't be worn by the lower classes. This law outraged the merchants and lower class. They rebelled by covering their bodies with illustrations that began at the neck and extended to the elbow on the arms and right above the knee on the legs."

Terry braced his arms on the table. "The people who rebelled would hide the tattoos beneath their clothing so as not to be punished by the ruling class. The underground tattooists flourished. The yakuza, the Japanese gangsters, embraced the body illustration suit mostly because it was illegal, and it was a unified form of showing their rebellion. This is where we see a lot of the development of the meaning for the symbols. The yakuza used different types of body suits as symbols of character.

"I found that across the world, the practice of tattooing was mostly associated with barbarians. Tattoos were used to identify slaves, criminals, mercenaries, and sometimes used as punishment in the ancient cultures on the European continent. The Latin word used for tattoo in that time was 'stigma.'"

Derek frowned. "That must be where stigmata came from."

Terry nodded. "The ancient Romans used tattoos to brand their criminals. But then in their battles, they saw that the Britons wore tattoos as badges of honor. The Roman armies were said to admire their enemies' ferocity, which in turn led to the admiration of the symbolic tattoos they wore. The Roman armies then began to wear tattoos of their own. Roman doctors would perfect the art of application and removal during the Crusades of the eleventh and twelfth centuries. The Jerusalem cross was used as an identifying mark so that a Christian warrior would be given a proper Christian burial."

Derek watched as Terry reached into the opposite shirt pocket from his cell phone and pulled out a cigar, peeling off the cellophane as he continued his lecture.

"Then in the early eighteenth century, European sailors sailed out to the South and Central Pacific islands and found that the indigenous people used a flat chisel-shaped piece of bone to tattoo. They would dip the sharp end of the bone in pigment made from soot and water. Then they would tap it with a mallet to embed the pigment into the skin."

He took the tip of the cigar and rolled it around in his mouth. "They also traded guns for the tattooed heads of Māori warriors."

Terry fished in his pants pocket and pulled out a cutter. "In 1891, the electric tattoo machine was invented. A few years later, American circuses hired people with full-body tattoos." He cut the end of his cigar. "They could earn a lot of money back then."

"I read about that on the internet." Derek watched as the tip of the cigar dropped onto his empty plate.

Terry waved the cigar in his hand. "From the 1930s to the '70s, tattoos weren't accepted in mainstream America. They were mostly worn by sailors and military men. Then in 1990 or '91, they found a 5,000-year-old ice man in the mountains between Austria and Italy. The ice man was so well preserved that the skin was still on the corpse. I've seen some pictures of it. The archeologists said that the skin of the ice man had over fifty-seven tattoos on it. One of the tattoos was a cross inside of one of his knees and lines around his ankles. They said that the tattoos might have been for a therapeutic reason for something like arthritis.

"Then I think it was around 1948 or so, they found some tombs between Russia and China. They found a bunch of mummies with tattoos. The tattoos that they had were of animals and magical monsters. These types of tattoos represent the status of the individuals wearing them and may have some type of magical significance."

"Wow, you sure know a lot." Derek sipped his tea.

"That's not even the half of it." Terry jammed the unlit cigar back in his mouth.

Derek threw his napkin onto his empty plate. "Yeah, it makes me realize that this is not just a bunch of pictures painted on me, that there is a real story being told here, and I have to figure out what that is."

"You may be right about that. When people come in and want a tattoo, some of the first questions we ask them are: *Where do you want it? How much do you want to spend? What type of tattoo are you going to get?*"

"Do you ever tell them that these things are permanent or ask if they have second thoughts?" Derek wondered.

"No." Terry took the cigar out of his mouth. "But if we hear them say something that doesn't sound right, like they're doing it to piss off their parents or they want to profess their undying love to a new girlfriend or boyfriend, we send them packing. Tell them to come back in a week and if they still feel that strongly about what they're doing then we'll accommodate their request."

"What if someone is intoxicated?" Derek persisted.

"Yeah, we'll do it." A shrug. "If they're walking and talking and still have the wherewithal, why not?"

"Because it seems to me that's when people are most likely to make a hasty decision. I would think that would be when most of the unwanted tattoos are made."

"Yeah, well you're probably right, but I'm not these people's keeper. Believe me, if they're making a decision like getting a tattoo while they're intoxicated, then they're making a lot bigger mistakes."

"That isn't the point," Derek protested.

"What is the point?" Terry jammed the cigar back in his mouth.

Derek shrugged. "It's just that it can be a very expensive mistake, both financially and emotionally."

"Yeah, I agree." Terry stood. "So the moral of the story is, if you walk into a tattoo parlor, you better have taken the time to think it through."

Derek smiled ruefully. "Thanks, Terry. You've been very informative." He stood and reached out to shake his hand. "I really appreciate that you took the time to explain this stuff to me."

Terry shook his inked hand. He grabbed the tattooing magazine off the table, rolled it, and tapped Derek on the arm. "It's my favorite subject."

Derek sat back down to finish his iced tea. Through the window, he saw Terry stop outside the café to light his cigar. He took a puff, then stood looking up and down the street as the cloud of smoke drifted off. A moment later, he disappeared into his shop.

Chapter 11

Brutus's incessant talking could be heard from behind the sunbaked apartment door as Derek approached. Using the spare key to enter, he gently greeted the bird to reassure him that he was not an unwelcome intruder.

Deeply absorbed in thought, he grabbed a beer from the tiny refrigerator. On his way out to the patio, he stopped to flip the switch for the ceiling fan. For a moment, he stood transfixed, watching the blades slowly build speed.

It surprised him how naturally he had fallen into Kendal's routine. Her relaxed lifestyle was a dramatic departure from his orderly routine. He wasn't sure if he was feeling so comfortable in her small apartment because of her hospitality or his dire circumstances. He and Kendal had been sharing a lot of personal information that would never have been discussed in the office.

He had felt her pain. He was curious what she was thinking. It was beginning to feel more like a friendship. He understood that Kendal was protecting her identity as an independent woman by trying to live true to her values, even though sometimes he threatened that.

It seemed they had entered a new place in their relationship. He was genuinely starting to admire Kendal. He understood that he needed to keep their newfound friendship in perspective by not taking advantage of her generous nature. She inspired him to be a better person. But it was hard to understand and share her feelings. He really needed to concentrate on figuring out how to save himself.

He stepped out into the sunshine on the deck. Closed his eyes and lifted his face toward the sun. He breathed in slowly through his nose, allowing his chest and stomach to rise as he filled his lungs. He exhaled slowly through his mouth. He felt the fatigue. His brain ached from the nonstop thinking.

Taking a swig of his beer, Derek stood at the railing, staring out at the horizon. He flashed back to the dream where he was trapped inside his high school. When he looked out between the threads of the web that stretched across the front doors, he could see the evil-eyed demons waiting.

He took a hard swig, but the beer couldn't wash away the fear. Pacing the length of the rail, Derek remembered another recurring nightmare that terrified him. He was in the school woodshop. He could hear the banging of lockers and yelling in the hallway as they came toward him. He hid behind the closed door, wishing he could feel the comfort and shelter of his grandmother's arms, as he had done when his father had passed away.

Then the demons burst into the room. Panic-stricken, he always woke in a cold sweat.

Looking down into his empty beer bottle, he saw the one nightmare that would always cut him to the core. The demons huddled in a circle, focused on something on the ground. They stepped back to reveal his grandmother, looking up pleadingly. His eyes connected with hers as the stick whistled down. He screamed—

"Hey, you, what are you doing out here?" Kendal stepped out onto the deck still wearing her scrubs.

Derek nearly jumped out of his skin. "Oh, my Lord, you just about gave me a heart attack." He clutched his chest.

"Sorry. I thought you heard me come in. So, what are you doing out here?"

"Ah, just thinking. Anything new at the office I should know about?" Derek deflected.

"No, nothing new. Most of the patients accept that you're having a family emergency. For the people who aren't willing to wait, I've been able to reschedule with Dr. Lee or Dr. Brock."

"What about the staff? Is anyone starting to get concerned?"

"No. I don't think so. We're all too busy."

"Thank you, Kendal." He gave her a grateful smile. "You don't know how much pressure this takes off not having to worry about the practice."

"Of course." She smiled back, radiant. "I'm happy to help. Did you get anything accomplished today?"

"Yeah, Dr. Cole gave me a lot to think about." Derek pushed his cap back on his head. "I was doing my homework when you came in. She wants me to start rebuilding my subconscious with new information."

"What kind of new information?" Kendal looked puzzled.

"Before I get into it, go change your scrubs and I'll get you something to drink."

"Sure, I'll be right back." Kendal disappeared inside.

She came back dressed in workout clothes. She climbed into

the adjacent chair, pulled her legs to her chest, then scooped up the glass of ice water Derek had waiting. "Where were we? Oh yeah . . . what new information?"

"She wants me to start rebuilding my subconscious."

"How?" She took a sip of her water.

"By rethinking my past. Rebuilding my belief system." Derek looked down at his hands. "I need to start analyzing my successes by looking at the paths that I took to get to where I am now."

"That sounds positive."

"It's going to be hard to set my misery aside and minimize the role that the attackers played. I realize that placing all the blame on other people can be an easy way to continue my negative behavior." He slumped further down into his chair.

"I don't think Dr. Cole expects you to forget about the people who hurt you. Maybe once you focus on the positive, the negative might not play such an important role."

"I can see how much better life is going to be not having to think about them anymore."

She nodded. "I think it's about taking control back."

"That would be nice. Lately I haven't felt like I have control over anything."

With a far-off look, Kendal brushed back a strand of hair. "The first time I felt like I had some control over my own destiny is when I moved here to California."

"That's understandable." Derek cocked his head. "You were young and running from abusive parents."

"I could never let my guard down. There were no boundaries in my home. I never felt safe."

"I'm sorry you had to go through that. I know how it feels to never feel safe."

They locked eyes, but it was a comfortable moment with none of their former awkwardness.

"Did the doctor give you any other exercises?"

Derek crossed his arms. "She also wants me to look at my tattoos as a positive and take time before I go to sleep to reconstruct my thought process."

"That sounds like a good idea," Kendal said cheerfully. "Where is it going to get you to *not* like your body, right?"

Derek sighed. "I haven't thought of it that way. To be honest, I've been thinking of these things as a foreign invader." He rubbed his hand across his forearm.

"Then maybe it's time to start looking at them as a part of your body and try to understand why they are there and what they mean to you."

"That's what I was doing today when I went over to the tattoo shop."

Kendal sat forward. "Oh, yeah, Terry called me, the guy who owns the tattoo shop."

"I know." A grin. "I was sitting right there."

"Then why did he call me?" She relaxed back into her chair.

"He didn't believe me when I told him that someone hadn't done all this work. He thought I was trying to pull a joke on him."

She laughed. "Oh, that's priceless."

"He needed some type of confirmation."

"Well, did it work?"

"Yes, he served time in the military. He's traveled all over the world. He gave me a lot of historical information and some of the symbolism."

"Did that help you to find some answers about what your tattoos mean?"

"No. Not really."

"It will. I'm sure this is all going to come together." She scooted forward in her chair. "Look, why don't you come to my kickboxing class tonight? I'm allowed to bring a guest."

Derek felt tempted. "It's been forever since I had a decent workout. Did you happen to grab any sweats from my house?"

"Yes, check out the bottom of the bag." She stepped back into the apartment.

"When do you want to leave?" he called.

"I still have about twenty minutes, and it only takes five to get there. So as long as you don't primp too much, we should be fine," she yelled from her bedroom.

"I'll try to control myself." He found his bag by the side of the couch and pulled out the clothes. "Hey, you want to ride the bike over there?"

"Sure," she said, coming back out to the living room.

"Does this mean you think I am a good rider?" he teased.

"It didn't look like you were going to fall off or anything. But I thought you said you didn't have a girlfriend." She propped her hands on her hips.

"I don't. Why?" He pulled his shirt off.

She pointed to the table that sat by the front door. "The extra helmet fits perfect."

He glanced over. "That doesn't mean I wasn't hoping for a

girlfriend." He locked eyes with her. "It pays to be prepared. I bought two helmets when I bought the bike. A guy never knows when some sweet young thing will want to take a ride on the back."

She held his gaze. "Am I a sweet young thing?"

"You can be, if you take a ride on the back of my bike."

Kendal chuckled and brushed past. "I think I had better get a jacket. This sweet young thing doesn't want to get cold."

"Especially after a workout," Derek grinned. "You don't want to catch a chill coming back!"

Chapter 12

Kendal wrapped her arms around his waist, trying not to hold on too tight. Riding on the back of Derek's motorcycle somehow felt intimate. Every twist of his wrist and she could feel her endorphins heighten.

The gym parking lot was full when they arrived. Kendal climbed off the back of the bike, took off the helmet, and fluffed her hair. "Come on, I'll introduce you to the instructor."

The activity inside came to a grinding halt as the pair walked in. A wave of awareness drifted across the room, with all eyes shifting to the front to get a look at the illustrated man.

"Wow, you really get people's attention," she muttered wryly. "It never gets old."

Derek shot her an exasperated look.

"I've brought a guest tonight," Kendal said to the instructor as he approached.

"I can see that." He held out a hand. "Hey, I'm Scott. Have you ever done any kickboxing before?"

"Yes, I've taken some classes," Derek replied, clasping his hand.

"Great! Sign in at the desk and then why don't you two go over and warm up?" Scott pointed to the far corner in the room. "We'll start sparring in about ten minutes."

Most of the people in the room had gone back to what they were doing, except for a small group that huddled in the adjacent corner.

"I'm heading over to say hello," Kendal whispered. "I just need to acknowledge these guys so they don't get weird on me."

"Weird on you?" Derek repeated with a quizzical look.

"I'll explain later," she said over her shoulder as she walked away.

Kendal knew that this little make-believe gang was only pretending to warm up. They started to huddle as she approached.

Kendal gave them a friendly wave.

Joe stepped out from the group; she knew he considered himself their leader.

"Who's the freak, Kendal?" Joe demanded in a nasty tone.

"Come on, Joe, is that any way to be?" she asked with a frown. "I nursed you over the years for all your little scrapes and bruises. I wouldn't say that to you if you brought in a friend."

"Yeah, well I'd never bring a freak like that into the club." He stood with his legs apart and hands on his hips.

"Okay, I think you should dial it down a notch," she said with a stern face.

The other guys inched closer, getting Joe's back.

Derek had been watching the group from across the room. He put down the jump rope. "Kendal, is everything okay?"

"Ah, darn," she muttered. "Everything is good!"

"What are you going to do about it if it's not?" Joe shouted at Derek across the room, apparently feeling brave with his buddies' support.

"Since when do you act like this, Joe?" Kendal chided.

Joe's eyes darkened. He clearly remembered her rebuff when he asked her to go out for a beer. "Since you started being a bitch—bringing your freaks into the gym."

"That is not an acceptable way to talk to anyone," she said, scowling now. "Would you like to take that back?"

"Who are you calling a bitch?" Derek shouted.

He strode across the gym. Joe looked at him, half smug and half uncertain as he contemplated his impending fate. Derek took two giant steps, jumped up and kicked Joe in the chest. He slammed him down to the mat as his buddies fell back to watch. Derek pinned Joe with a forearm to the throat. "Is there anything else you have to say?"

"No," Joe mumbled. He drew a panting breath before closing his eyes to block out the inked face.

"Apologize to the lady," Derek said flatly.

Kendal tapped Derek's shoulder. "Come on, you've made your point."

"No. He called you a bitch. You don't speak to a lady that way. Kendal, you deserve an apology."

"I think I just got one," Kendal said firmly. "Let's go."

"No," he said, this time even more stern. "Apologize to the lady."

Joe took a deep breath and looked up at Kendal. "I apologize," he said tightly. "For calling you a bitch."

"Apology accepted," Kendal said.

The bubble of tension popped. Derek released him and stood. The group circled Joe. He scowled, shoving one of his buddies, and stormed off. Kendal took Derek's arm. "Let's get out of here," she suggested.

"I'm sorry," Derek said in a subdued tone as they approached the Harley.

"Why? It's not your fault. He's the one who should be sorry. I've been nothing but nice to those losers."

"So . . . what do you want to do now that I screwed everything up for you?"

Kendal smiled. "You didn't screw anything up for me. You were just trying to help, I get it."

He grinned slightly. "Do you really think so?"

"Absolutely. It kind of felt good having that sort of protection."

"Well, I think it's only fair that you get to decide where we go tonight," he said.

She turned away and climbed onto the back of the bike. "Let's go down to the beach."

Kendal held on to his back tightly as he revved the engine and pulled out. As they drove past the tall, elegant buildings and palm trees in the distance, amidst the backdrop of a beautiful summer night, her mood began to shift. The purr of the Harley and feeling of Derek's body against hers were both exciting and relaxing. They cruised into the empty beach parking lot. Kendal sat leaning against his back, watching the waves roll in.

Derek lifted the shield of his helmet. "You know it's hard to be labeled like this," he said, looking pensively at the horizon.

"I know it is."

Derek took his helmet off and set it on the handlebars. "I could understand if I were exhibiting a deviant behavior or attitude, but it seems crazy that people would have such a visceral response to tattoos." He seemed to be talking more to himself than to her.

"You know, it's a cultural thing," she said.

"How is it a cultural thing?"

She laughed. "People look around and see people. They see individuals who look just like them, and they want everybody in society to stay that way."

"But that's it. These tattoos are overwhelming my identity. I'm not who I'm supposed to be."

Kendal looked at him and rubbed his back. "Well, I like your new identity. Gives you a kind of sick look."

Derek burst out laughing. "Sick look? What's that supposed to mean?"

Kendal started laughing, too. "You know, like cool!"

"Cool? You think these tattoos on my face look cool? Let's be honest. I look like a former prison inmate who couldn't catch a break."

The two of them began laughing hysterically. "I mean, you seriously think I look good like this?" Derek wheezed.

Kendal caught her breath. She looked straight into his eyes. "Yes, as a matter of fact. On you, I think they look very cool."

"Uh, you mean sick, right?" he said, grinning widely.

They started laughing again.

"Yes, that's exactly what I mean! And don't forget, the doctor said you should embrace the change."

She climbed off the back of the bike with her helmet under her arm and stood to face him. "You must make this condition work for you. That's why it is important for you to find out the meaning of these tattoos." She put her hand on his. "That will give you your power back."

"Can you see me in a business suit again?" he wondered. "Or in my doctor's scrubs? People would either run or stand there and laugh."

"Don't be so dramatic—"

"You saw what just happened!"

"There's more going on than you know about. Joe was jealous because I turned him down. He would have hated *any* guy I brought around." She smiled. "It was more about me than it was about your tattoos—those guys were just being punks."

"They're the tip of the iceberg," Derek muttered.

Kendal put her arm around his shoulder, hoping to cheer him up. "You know, before this happened I could never imagine you with a tattoo."

He turned to face her. "Really?"

"You had that boy-next-door look, so cute with the blond hair and blue eyes."

"You're saying I'm not cute anymore?" He feigned a sulky look.

"You're good-looking but in a different way. You seem adventurous. You don't look like you need to play by anyone else's rules. More rugged and masculine, I guess."

"I wasn't rugged and masculine before?"

"I think you're more of a Ryan Gosling type. You still have the boyish charm, but now you're kind of a bad ass. Especially after what you pulled off at the gym." She grinned. "Remember, he rides a motorcycle too."

Their eyes locked. Derek looked away first. "It's getting a bit chilly," he said as he put his helmet back on.

Kendal felt a little self-conscious and confused by his reaction. She put her helmet on while watching Derek walk the bike backwards turning the wheel as it rolled back around behind her.

"Get on." He flipped the shield of his helmet back down.

She carefully stepped up on the peg, straddled the seat, and wrapped her arms securely around his chest. "Let's go home," she called out from beneath her helmet.

Kendal lay in bed that evening feeling helpless as she listened to Derek's fitful cries of anguish throughout the night.

Chapter 13

Dr. Cole glanced up from the cream-colored folder, light green eyes framed by her thick-rimmed glasses. Derek had just completed another session of recounting his childhood traumas. Now he sat waiting for her to finish checking her notes. He'd promised Kendal he would make a concerted effort to listen and understand the doctor's conclusions, but he knew it would take time.

Dr. Cole closed the folder and adjusted her glasses. "One of the things you need to consider, Dr. Hollinger, is that you are not the person you were originally destined to be. That was taken from you the day you were assaulted. The normal progression of emotional development was interrupted by a truly traumatic and violent act."

She set the file down. "This traumatic event, coupled with the pain of multiple surgeries, physical therapy, as well as the loss of your childhood, would definitely contribute to your post-traumatic stress disorder. These tattoos or stigmata could be an expression of that pain."

The doctor removed her glasses, regarding him with sympathy. "The reason why I have come to this conclusion is that you have stated you are reliving the events in your dreams, and you seem to have guilt regarding the death of your grandmother. The symptoms increase when things are stressful."

"You mean like when I wake up in the morning covered in tattoos?" Derek asked.

She ignored the jibe. "It's normal to have a wide range of feelings, but the PTSD symptoms can become so bad that emergency treatment is required. This can permanently affect your mental health. The extreme beating you suffered was life-threatening in more ways than just the physical attack. Your symptoms have manifested in quite a distinct way."

He exhaled a calming breath. "So my question is still the same. How do I get rid of this problem?"

She set the glasses on her desk. "Let me remind you, I cannot solve the mystery of how you came to have these tattoos. My job is to help you resolve or change the negative emotions attached to the tattoos. Ask yourself, what do you see when you look in the mirror? What is the meaning of the tattoos? How do they connect?"

Derek stared at her. He had a few guesses, but not enough to form a coherent answer. It was like an archaeologist trying to piece together the history of a lost civilization based on a few shards of pottery—or a handful of faded cave drawings. The silence lengthened.

"I believe we *are* making progress," Dr. Cole said at last in an encouraging voice. "Come back and see me at the same time tomorrow. Don't hesitate to call if you have any questions."

Derek left feeling frustrated. He swung a leg over the motorcycle seat. "My brain has been turned inside out for the entire world to see," he muttered. "Yet no one seems to understand what the heck my subconscious is trying to say!"

He downshifted, then rode to his office. He parked on the street and sat looking up at the building, head spinning. "My time is a precious commodity," he fumed. "And I'm not making any progress!"

He'd thought he was on the right path to figuring out how to get rid of the tattoos. But Dr. Cole had made it clear today that was not *her* primary focus. He tugged his baseball cap down snug on his head, strode purposefully through the front doors, and headed straight for the elevator. At the twentieth floor, a woman and her little girl stepped out into the hall just in time to face a tattooed man. The mother's jaw tightened. She grabbed her daughter's hand and tugged her away.

Derek opened the door to his office and found an empty waiting room. The receptionist, Nicole, sat behind the mahogany desk, typing on a computer. "Can I help you?" she asked without looking over.

"Yes. I want to talk to Kendal."

The unexpected familiarity of the voice made Nicole look up. Her eyes widened. "Kendal?" she echoed.

Derek leaned over the desk. "Who else would I be talking about?"

Nicole stood and backed away from the desk, bumping into Kendal as she approached.

"It's okay," Kendal said quickly, taking Derek's arm and pulling him aside. "What are you doing here?" she hissed. "You didn't tell me you were coming."

It was all too much. "Why wouldn't I be here? I have a right to be here just like anyone else. Actually, *more* than anyone else!"

Derek heard his voice rising and tried to calm down.

"Excuse us, Nicole," Kendal said briskly. She placed both hands on his chest and pushed him back out into the hall.

"What do you think you're doing?" he protested.

"Me? What are *you* doing?" Kendal demanded. She glanced over her shoulder and made sure the lobby door was closed behind them. "You're going to ruin everything. Why are you here? Do you want your partners to find out?"

"I don't think I care anymore." Derek gritted his teeth.

"Yes, you do," she replied, clearly striving for patience. "What's gotten into you? I thought you were going to see the doctor this morning."

He leaned against the wall. "I did."

"So what happened?" Kendal studied his face.

A couple walked toward them, gawking. Derek faked a lunge towards the man. The couple spun and took off in a half walk, half run down the hall, looking back over their shoulders to make sure they weren't being followed.

"*That* was mature." Kendal stepped closer. Lowering her voice, she asked, "Why are you acting this way?"

"Because I'm fed up! I can't stand this anymore." He grabbed the bill of his cap, lifting it and then yanking it back down again in frustration.

"Keep your voice down." She put a finger to her lips.

"I need answers," he said with a note of desperation.

"Well, this sure isn't the way to do it." She frowned. "There's too much at stake, Derek."

"I can't just continue to hang around." He looked up the hall.

"Look, we're trying to figure this out. That's why you went to see Dr. Cole. Believe me," she made eye contact with him, "I'm not going to let you lose your business. Just stay calm."

"Holy crap!" He let out a long sigh. "I don't know how much longer I can take this. I feel like I'm losing my mind."

"No, you're not," she said firmly. "I'm not going to let you. You are not alone."

"Really?" He looked down at the floor. "Why would you want to be involved in this craziness?" He shoved his hands deep into his front pockets. "What do you get out of this?"

Kendal's eyes widened in disbelief.

"Why would you want to get involved with me?" He hung his head in shame. "Look at me, I'm a mess."

"I am looking at you through your heart." She laid her hand on his chest.

Derek cupped his hand over her hand. "I don't know what I would do without you." Lifting her hand, he kissed the palm and walked away.

"See you at home," Kendal called out.

Derek put his thumb up in the air, not turning around.

The bellman stood outside the hotel. Derek parked his motorcycle off to one side.

"Hello, sir," the bellman said, avoiding eye contact.

"I need to ask you a couple of questions."

The regally dressed doorman stood silent.

"There was an old woman with tattoos on her face here

Saturday night. A man was getting out of his car and she approached him. He knocked her down, did you see that?"

He shook his head.

He slipped the doorman a ten-dollar bill. "Well, I'm looking for the old woman to make sure she's okay. Have you seen her?"

"No, sir. I have not."

"Had you seen her before that night?"

"No, sir. That was the first time. I haven't seen her since. The hotel does not allow vagrants to hang out down here."

"If you see her, would you give me a call?"

"Sure."

Derek handed him his business card.

"Dr. Derek Hollinger?" the doorman read out loud.

"He's a friend of mine."

"Yes, sir," the man said doubtfully.

"Just call that number if you should see her, okay?"

The man nodded—and seemed friendlier when Derek handed him another ten-dollar bill.

"Have a good evening, sir!" he called, as Derek walked to his bike.

Derek spent the next hour riding up and down the adjacent streets, hoping to catch the old woman walking around the area or panhandling on a corner. He would stop to talk to the homeless, describe the old woman, give a couple dollars, then move to the next location. But she'd vanished into thin air.

He pulled up at Kendal's apartment complex just as she was arriving home.

"Perfect timing!" she called out, hair flying from beneath her fedora.

Her happy face gave him a flutter. He couldn't help but return the smile.

"Where have you been?" Kendal unlocked the gate and Derek pushed it open.

"I went out looking for the old shaman woman."

"Any luck?"

"No. I talked to a lot of people, but no one has seen her."

"I wonder if they were people working the area, you know, like gypsies, panhandlers that travel around the country. They don't stay in one place for very long."

"Well, that would make sense because I am coming up empty."

"Come on and have a beer, sounds like you've earned it."

At the top of the stairs, Kendal opened the door. Brutus began to whistle and screech.

"Hello, Brutus," she said fondly.

The bird ran back and forth along his perch.

Derek set his helmet and gloves on the end table, took his leather jacket off and hung it up by the door. He sat down in the chair and pulled off his boots. Kendal handed him the beer, then opened the sliding door to let the ocean breeze in. She flipped the switch for the ceiling fan, and it began to turn slowly. Sitting down on the couch she stretched her legs out across the cushions.

With his feet perched on the coffee table, Derek said, "Wow, I never in a million years thought that I would be sitting in a tiny little apartment down by the beach sipping beer."

"Really?" She smiled. "What did you imagine you would be doing?"

He shrugged. "I'm just saying that I'm used to a different kind of lifestyle."

"You don't drink beer, or you don't sit in tiny little apartments?" she teased.

He gave her a mock scowl. "That's not what I meant. I just mean it's different. That's all."

Chapter 14

Kendal pulled her car into the public lot. It was emptied out for the day. The beach was deserted except for two kids playing in the surf and a man walking his dog a hundred yards down the sand.

The sun dipped behind a low cloud as they approached the water's edge. It was the first day of the new moon. The solitude of the rolling waves with the shifting sand seemed to wash the world's troubles away.

Derek took a deep breath, watching the sun sink behind the horizon. "I am a very lucky man to have such a wonderful woman like you for my friend." He took her hand. "Thank you."

Later, he would discover that the tattooed chains around his ankles had disappeared.

Derek reached out for her. She submitted instantly, a bit confused as to why she was giving in so quickly. She had seen the volatile side of him again and it still scared her. She'd run fast and hard to get away from that type of guy. Yet somehow, in her heart, she knew Derek was different. He had been traumatized at such a young age and spent the rest of his life building a hard shell to protect himself. Maybe that shell was finally cracking.

The kiss was long and passionate. They stood at the water's edge until dark, then hugged each other lazily and made their way back to the car. Kendal zipped into a parking spot in front of the pub next to the tattoo shop.

"Let's stop for a drink," she suggested light-heartedly.

The lights were dim. Music played on the jukebox. A pool table sat in the middle of the room. The ringing of a pinball machine came from the back of the bar.

"What would you like?" Derek asked.

"Oh, just a glass of wine, whatever they have. Red."

Derek passed a group at a small table on his way to the large horseshoe bar. Kendal went in the opposite direction looking for a place to sit. As he approached, he could feel the intense stare of two guys sitting at the bar. He stood at the edge for a minute waiting for the barmaid. The woman glanced over, meandered down, and put a napkin on the bar.

"What can I get for you?" she asked, studying his face.

"The lady over there would like a glass of red wine and I'll have a beer on tap."

She dropped a second napkin in front of him and walked away. Moments later, she returned with a small glass of red wine and a mug of beer.

"You want to run a tab?"

"Sure."

"Credit card, please."

Derek pulled out his wallet, handed her his credit card, then grabbed the two drinks. He set them down on the small scarred dark wood table.

"Nice place," he mused sarcastically, looking around.

"You play pool?" Kendal asked.

"Yeah, but it's been a while. I used to play in college." He took a sip of his beer.

"Wow, you're right, it has been a while." She smiled.

"Hey, watch it." He frowned. "I'm not that old."

"Says who? You're twelve years older than me." She skipped past with a laugh, just out of his reach, and headed over to the pool table. She took some change out of her pocket as Derek watched, dropping the coins in the slot. Kendal pushed the handle. Balls came rolling down. Derek sat transfixed as she went to the front of the table, bent over, and racked the pool balls.

Kendal inspected her rack, then called out, "Break 'em!"

Shaken from his trance, Derek set his beer down. Trying to look confident, he picked out a stick. Kendal rolled her cue back and forth, checking to see if it was straight, and stood swaying to the music, waiting for Derek to make the first move.

He placed the cue ball on the felt at the end of the table, lined up the tip of his stick to the center of the ball, sharpened his stance, then hit the nose, full force. It rolled down the table and made a solid hit. The balls at the other end broke with a crack and rolled outward, but nothing sank.

"Not bad for an old timer," she teased.

Kendal analyzed the table for her shot. The first ball went into the pocket. The next shot required her to stretch across the table, extending her body so that she was up on one toe. When she hit the ball, it popped up into the air and hit the floor.

Derek chuckled and bent over to pick up the cue ball. As he stood, someone knocked his cap off. Derek ducked and raised his fists. "Hey man, what's your problem?" he demanded.

"You're not a doctor." It was one of the guys from the bar. "You came in here trying to scam my girlfriend . . . the barmaid out of her money. Where'd you get that credit card? You steal it?"

"That's none of your business," he replied flatly.

"It's *my* business when you're trying to pull one over on my girl."

Derek heard a man's voice from behind, "Yeah, you trying to pull one over on my buddy's girl?"

It was the second guy. He now had one in front and one behind.

He could see Kendal behind the first guy who had knocked off his cap. He calculated that she was far enough away if he had to take a swing. Then the guy behind him hit him square in the kidney. The blow brought him to his knees. In the corner of his eye, he saw Kendal make a move toward him. Someone grabbed her; she twisted around with a kick. Panic and fury made his pulse race. It was like the day after school. The day he was helpless, outnumbered, beaten to a bloody pulp . . .

He choked down the sour taste of fear. He had to save Kendal. It didn't matter what they did to him, but he had to protect her. In the edge of his vision, he saw two more guys. Scrambling to get up, he stumbled. One kicked him hard, and he heard Kendal scream as he went back down.

A piercing whistle got everyone's attention. Derek looked up to see all his attackers facing the front door. He rolled over, squinting through watery eyes. There in the doorway stood Terry.

"What's going on here?" Terry barked.

The boyfriend of the barmaid spoke up. "This guy is trying to pass himself off as a doctor. He stole a credit card and he's trying to use it, Terry. We plan on stopping him from ripping you off."

"He *is* a doctor, stupid," Terry growled, shaking his head.

"What? He's not a doctor, look at him."

"I know this guy. Help him up. NOW!" Terry commanded.

The two biggest guys stepped forward to help Derek to his feet. The one standing next to him picked up his cap, brushed it off, and handed it over with a sheepish look.

"Now get out of here. If I want your help, I'll ask for it. Go get a drink. JANIE!" Terry bellowed at the woman behind the bar. "Give these boys a drink, on me." He walked over and put his hand on Derek's shoulder. "Sorry about that, man."

Kendal came rushing over and gave him a hug. "Oh, my God, are you all right?"

Derek felt a warm rush at the contact. He gently disengaged himself from her embrace as Terry grinned at them both.

"Yeah, I'm fine. Just my ego that got a little bruised. I thought I was faster than that."

Chewing on his cigar stub, Terry said in a dry voice, "These boys get in a lot of fights. They've had a lot of practice, Doc."

"What brings you in here tonight?" Derek asked.

"I own this place."

"Really—this place, too?"

Kendal grabbed Derek's arm and shot him a look.

"Oh, Kendal this is Terry, Terry this is my good friend Kendal. This is the guy who owns the tattoo shop next door."

"Ah, you called me yesterday," she said.

Terry nodded. "I hope you were okay with that."

"Absolutely, we appreciate your help."

Terry winked. "Don't worry, his secret is safe with me. These dummies over here don't have a clue what's going on. They aren't going to say anything. All they care about is drinking, smoking, and women, in that order."

"Well, we had better get out of here before we start any more trouble. Thanks for the rescue." Derek shook his hand.

Kendal grabbed her jacket off the back of the chair, then stood at the bar with her hand out. The barmaid, Janie, ruefully put the credit card in Kendal's hand. Kendal helped Derek hobble out, still reeling from the kidney punch.

She opened the car door. Derek gingerly slipped into the front seat and looked up at her. "This is going to be my life, isn't it?"

"No." She closed the door and walked around to driver's side.

"I'm not going to be able to go anywhere without someone giving me grief." He stared out the windshield.

"This isn't the time to be thinking about that kind of stuff." Kendal started the car.

Derek turned his head. "Then when is the time?"

"A bar fight is not a good representation of your future." She shifted into reverse, a smile tugging at the corner of her mouth. "Now maybe you'd be feeling a little better if you had *won* the fight."

Derek looked over, amused. "You think I can't fight?"

"I know you can fight. I just wonder how you would be in a *real* fight."

"Okay, you're on. I can't wait to see what you think *real* fighting is."

Kendal pulled up to the curb in front of her apartment, jumped out of the car and helped Derek get out.

"This is going to sting for a while," he muttered ruefully.

"I'm sure it is." Kendal put her arm around his waist.

They made their way slowly across the courtyard and around the pool. Kendal raced up the steps to open the door and waited for him to enter the apartment. He slowly lowered himself into the oversized rattan chair.

"Terry seems like a pretty nice guy, and he seems to like you." Kendal sank down to the couch across from Derek.

"He is really into his craft, that's for sure."

"Maybe you could have him look at your tattoos and see what he thinks the meaning might be," she suggested.

"I think that's a really good idea. Maybe he'll have some insight on what relation they have to each other and how they are placed."

"If anybody could, I think it would be him."

"Terry says it's the sports stars and celebrities that are influencing the trend."

She smiled and wiggled one foot. "I don't think I'd have gotten this one on my ankle if I hadn't seen so many on famous women. Seeing how cool they look made me want to have one."

"Let me see it," Derek said.

Kendal slipped off her sandal and braced her bare foot on his thigh. Derek curled a hand around her leg and examined the sun tattoo. Her skin felt like warm silk beneath his fingers. He cleared his throat.

"Why did you get it on your ankle?" he asked.

She arched a brow. "Because I didn't want a 'tramp stamp' on my back to show off with low-cut jeans."

"I see." He smiled. "You *do* worry about what people think."

"I guess a little bit," she admitted. "I just wanted to be a little more discreet about it. Not draw too much attention."

He traced the outline with one finger, the way she had done to him. "So why did you pick the sun?"

"Because the sun is what brought me to California. It represents going from dark times to seeing the light. It reminds me to be happy."

"That's pretty cool," Derek said. "Simple and sweet."

Kendal withdrew her leg. "I thought so."

He leaned back. "Terry's right. People get tattoos for different reasons. They have an individualistic meaning to each person. It's such a subjective art."

"But you didn't have the intent and meaning preconceived like most people."

"Exactly." He frowned. "It's kind of like reading the ending of a book first. And speaking of books, did you see that I have a book with some writing on my back? Maybe you could look and tell me what it says. The letters are too small for me to read."

"Sure," Kendal agreed.

Derek slowly peeled his shirt off. His kidney still ached from the brutal punch he had taken earlier.

"Come sit on the couch so I can look at it by the light," Kendal said.

She leaned closer. Her breath tickled his neck.

"Hold on," she said. "I have a magnifying glass in the drawer."

A minute later, she held the magnifying glass to the tattoo.

"It's the Bible," she said.

That surprised him. "Really?"

"I think I can read a little bit." She paused. "It says, 'The gates of Jericho were kept tightly shut because the people were afraid.'"

Derek felt a flash of confusion. "That's the story of the Walls of Jericho my grandmother used to read to me from the Bible. I remember that was one of her favorite stories."

"Huh. That is really cool."

"I wonder what it means?" he muttered softly.

Kendal set the magnifying glass aside. "You have so many tattoos. You should start taking them one at a time. Try to get the meaning and any association you can possibly think of to see if some type of pattern or blueprint emerges."

"That's a good idea. I should've done it a while ago."

He felt a pang of regret as she rose to her feet and walked to her bedroom. "I hope you sleep better. I hear you at night."

His cheeks burned with embarrassment. "Oh man, I'm sorry! I'm keeping you awake."

"Don't be sorry, Derek. I just feel for you. I know you're trying so hard to figure this thing out. Let me know if you need anything." She smiled. "Good night."

He smiled back, wishing she would stay. "Good night, Kendal."

The door closed.

Derek was getting ready for bed when he noticed that the chain on his right ankle was no longer there. He looked up at the closed bedroom door and instantly wanted to call out Kendal's name but couldn't.

The insecurities started immediately. *I don't want to get my hopes up—or Kendal's. Are the tattoos starting to disappear? Why only one? Could it be connected to the kiss?* He thought he had felt something, a change.

He plopped down on the couch and stretched out. He tried to control his breath and relax.

Within a couple of minutes, Derek's childhood memories came flooding back. After his father passed away, he remembered his grandmother would read the Bible to him every night. Those Bible stories influenced his dreams before the violent beating created nightmares instead. He now realized that those essential stories had given him hope and faith that everything would be all right in the end. It helped him to focus during his time of grief. That one loving act of reading to him each night had been instrumental in molding his thinking.

He turned off the light and lay back to remember what his grandmother had told him about the story of Jericho. She had explained that the battle was to remind us that our enemy can't be destroyed with physical weapons. That God will fight for us. Derek drifted off to sleep with his grandmother's voice in his head.

Chapter 15

Kendal and Derek had fallen into a morning routine. Derek would rise at the break of dawn and make the coffee, then go out on the balcony and still be ruminating on his nightmares when Kendal stumbled out.

It was the first morning he woke refreshed since the whole ordeal began. When he opened his eyes, he was surprised to find that the sun was up. He had slept through the night without so much as a dream, good or bad, or none that he recalled at least.

Derek stood to get his second cup of coffee when Kendal came shuffling out.

"Good morning, sunshine," he said with a wide grin.

"Good morning, Doc."

"Coffee?"

"Sure."

Derek found Kendal's Disneyland cup hanging on the cup rack. He poured them both coffee and went back out to the balcony, where she sat stifling a yawn with one hand.

"Are you going into the office today?"

"Yes." She stretched. "I need to make sure that the scheduled surgeries go smoothly. If anyone's looking for you, I can divert them." She picked up her coffee and took a sip.

How beautiful she looked, with her hair softly tousled from sleep and one tanned shoulder poking out .

"Kendal," he said, his throat a little tight. "I can't imagine how I'd possibly be handling this without you."

She shrugged and blew on the coffee. "If I can keep your partners from getting too suspicious then everything should be okay. So far, they've been too busy focusing on taking care of the overflow to ask a lot of questions." She gave him a level look. "But at some point, they're going to expect to talk to you. So, I think you better start preparing for that conversation."

He nodded. "I know. I was thinking about it this morning. I should go in on Monday to talk to them."

Kendal sat straight up in her chair. "No. I don't think you should do it that soon. I can buy you more time. Let's see how this plays out. The more time you take, the more time you can prepare and protect yourself for the fallout."

"Maybe you're right." He sighed. "I keep going back and forth on what's my best move."

Kendal relaxed. "The best move is not to let them know anything for now. You know what type of people they are. They're going to take advantage of the crisis. They'll see it as an opportunity. I really don't see them being sympathetic." She studied his face. "But then again, up until this week, I don't think you would have been very sympathetic if this would have happened to one of them."

Kendal took a sip of her coffee, holding his gaze. Derek wanted to deny it, but he knew it was true.

"You're right," he said. "I had no tolerance or empathy unless I was getting paid for it. I guess that's not saying much for the type of person I am. And it sure doesn't say much for the people I've surrounded myself with."

"Not all the people."

He reached for her hand. "Not everybody. I have you. You're the exception to the rule."

"Thank you." She laughed. "Ah, it's too early to be getting upset."

"I definitely don't want you getting upset," he agreed. "How's the coffee this morning?"

"Good." She lifted her Disney mug into the air. "You're getting better at this, Doc."

"Better at what?"

"Better at making coffee." Another chuckle. "Why? What did you think I was going to say?"

"I thought you were going to tell me I'm getting better at apologizing."

"That too." She ran her hands through her hair. "So, what's on the agenda for today?"

"I'm going to Dr. Cole's office this morning. Then I think I should go looking for the old lady again."

The shaman, he thought. Derek wasn't sure if he was eager to find her—or terrified that he actually might.

"Stay in touch," Kendal said. "I may need to ask you some questions. We have surgeries today and I want to make sure I can get a hold of you if I need to."

"And I'll make sure I keep my cell phone on," he promised.

Kendal finished her last sip of coffee and went to the kitchen.

She set her cup in the sink and turned just as Derek reached past her to put his own cup in the sink. They both froze, bodies pressed together in the tiny space. Her gaze flicked down to his shorts then back to his face. Her cheeks warmed to an adorable pink.

"I can't go around," she said faintly. "Would you like me to go under you?"

"Hmm, that sounds nice," he whispered in her ear.

"Funny." Kendal put her hand on his chest and backpedaled him out of the kitchen into the living room. Then she kissed him on the shoulder and bolted past, closing her bedroom door.

Derek looked over at Brutus. "What are you so happy about this morning?"

The bird bobbed his head, then ran up and down on his perch screeching.

A few minutes later, Kendal came out dressed in scrubs with her hair pulled back. "See you later." She grabbed her keys and purse, hesitated at the front door, then turned and blew a kiss. "Remember, stay in touch in case I need you today."

"I will," He called out as the door closed behind her.

Derek walked over to the window. He watched the convertible pull away. Then he jumped into the shower, feeling better about life than he had in a long time.

Chapter 16

Derek checked in with Dr. Cole's receptionist. The young woman brought him back to the doctor's office immediately. She sat working in a pressed black suit, head down, surrounded by stacks of files—like a fortress around her desk.

Derek stood in front of her with his hands in his pockets.

She glanced up. "Good morning, Derek, have a seat." She laid her glasses on the desk. "How are you today?"

"Do all psychologists ask such moronic questions?" The aggravation he'd felt yesterday came surging back. "How do I look, doctor?"

"How does that question serve you?" she countered.

Derek sat down. "You should be able to see how I'm doing by the tattoos. That's why I'm here to see you, right?"

Her tone was maddeningly calm. "I was hoping that by this point you would be grasping the concept."

"Maybe I'm missing something." He leaned back in his chair.

She put the glasses back on, then pushed them up to her forehead. "You should be preparing yourself. What that means is you must be working to try to solve this, but at the same time working to be prepared for any outcome. Either way, you should be taking control of your destiny to be able to live a healthy, happy life."

He expelled a long breath through his nose.

"The only way you'll be able to do that," she continued, "is by facing the past, dealing with the present, and laying the foundation for your future. I believe this is what we are trying to accomplish in these sessions. What do you think you should be accomplishing here?"

"I think I want to get my life back," he muttered, staring out the half open blinds of the window behind her.

"What does that look like?" Her gaze softened.

"For one thing, I want to get my medical practice back."

"Is that it?"

Derek pulled his collar to get more air. "I want a relationship and friends."

"How are you going to accomplish that?"

"I believe I've already started. I have a friend now." He felt that familiar pang of longing.

Dr. Cole looked pleased. "And how are you going to expand on that friendship?"

"I guess I need to spend more time associating with other people besides my colleagues at work." Derek picked at a thread on his jeans.

"That sounds like a good start."

He lifted his gaze and looked directly at her. "The last few days, I've encountered some great people willing to give me their time and energy—and not because they are looking for something in return."

"How does that make you feel?"

He shrugged. "Like I have value that goes beyond what I do in my profession."

"Do you think you could start reciprocating in that type of relationship?" Dr. Cole leaned her chin on a hand, regarding him closely.

"What do you mean?"

"By giving people time and energy without expecting something in return."

"I haven't thought about it."

"Have you found that this type of lifestyle has left you feeling like something is missing?"

"Yes," he admitted, feeling his discomfort rising. "Now that I'm in a situation where I need people to help me."

"It sounds like you're starting to understand that you must have a healthy balance between your business life and spiritual life."

"When it comes to my spirit, I think I need to find the old woman who put this curse on me and have her reverse it."

Dr. Cole slowly shook her head. "You're wasting your time."

"Why? If I can get her to reverse it, then all of this can be over."

"How do you know if she agrees to reverse the curse that your subconscious is going to be willing to listen? After all, it is truly your subconscious that is in control of this—not the old woman."

He started to feel a throb in his head. "I still don't understand how she could have said the words, and *this* happened."

She raised her palms. "*What words*? You don't even know what those words are. Even if she spouted off some words at the time that you had the interaction with her, there is no way that she could have told you in such detail what was going to happen to you."

"So I did do this to myself?" His jaw tightened.

"The conditions that you were living under caused this to

happen, starting with the death of your father, the beating, the loss of your grandmother, the loss of all your friends, finally the reclusive life since the loss of your mentor." She leaned forward. "I must say, you've created a remarkable defense mechanism, Dr. Hollinger."

Derek's eyes narrowed. "How in the world can you call this a *defense mechanism?*"

"It seems to be a type of shield. You've been exhibiting stress disorder symptoms and have tried to cope with them on your own. Some people end up in mental institutions because of the toll it takes on them."

Her voice gained confidence. "Through the years, you have buried the bad emotions and focused on your profession. Encountering the old shaman woman on that day was your tipping point. Your subconscious couldn't take anymore, and it had to have some type of release to manifest all the pent-up emotions. I believe that this is how your subconscious, your spirit, has decided to deal with your anxieties and pain—by displaying them on your skin. At this point, you are going to have to focus on forgiveness."

"Who do I have to forgive?" he asked, tapping his fingers on the chair.

She smiled. "You can start with yourself . . . or anyone who hasn't done right by you. Anyone who has physically harmed you. Or someone you loved that hurt you." She hesitated. "Maybe even *God.*"

He curled his hands around the chair arms. "I don't know the people who almost beat me to death. I mean, I didn't even know I was mad at God."

"Maybe mad isn't quite the right word. But I'm sure you had questions about why this happened to you."

"Yes, all the time." He rubbed his leg, trying to comfort himself.

"That's my point. Then you don't think that it's something that was supposed to happen, correct?"

He crossed his arms tightly. "Who thinks that they deserve to be beaten half to death?"

With a neutral expression, she asked, "Then who do you blame?"

Derek shrugged. "Mostly, my mom, I guess . . . for causing me to walk home alone. Then the guys who jumped me."

"That's it?"

"No, I guess I do feel like fate has dealt me an unfair blow with the death of my father and the loss of my grandmother, the beating . . ." He pressed two fingers against his aching temple. "I feel like this manifestation of tattoos all over my body has just added insult to injury."

"Who do you ultimately blame?"

Derek grimaced. "I guess you *could* say God . . . although I lost my faith in both humanity and the divine a long time ago. No one cared about me. Why should I care about them?"

"Do you hear how that type of thinking could lead you to this place?" Dr. Cole asked gently.

"No." His mouth twisted. "I don't think I should be sitting here with tattoos all over my body because I haven't been praying to God every Sunday."

"That's not what I'm saying." She tilted her head, gaze intent.

"What I am saying is that you haven't been balancing yourself. You haven't been nourishing your soul. You blocked off one section of your being, the spiritual side, to people and to the flow of life. You had emotional congestion. Everything has built up to the point of needing to have an outlet or release. If you continue to entertain such negative thoughts toward God and humankind in general, you will continue to experience automatic negative reactions from your subconscious."

Derek closed his eyes. "Go on."

"You are going to have to find a way to release the resentment, anger, and hostility. The act of violence that was perpetrated on you seems to have been a random act, just as you have described it. The early passing of your father was an unfortunate life event and not a predestined punishment of you. The passing of your grandmother may have been directly related to the events at that time, but you know as well as I do she may have been suffering from a pre-existing ailment."

"Fair enough," he muttered.

"So the guilt and anger you have carried about her should be turned into loving memories of a woman who loved you and shared many long hours of happiness. You must focus on the happy times. Remember to forgive yourself first. Then you can start to forgive everyone else."

Something loosened in his chest. Like a dam suddenly breaking wide. Derek began to sob. "I caused my grandmother to die," he whispered, hands shaking. "If I would have gone home when I was supposed to, those guys would not have found me walking alone that day."

Dr. Cole handed Derek a tissue. "You have been transformed by your early childhood experiences. It obviously started with the damage perpetrated on your physical being, which in turn shattered your psychological and emotional well-being. It's all right to be sad. This has really been hard on you."

He wiped his eyes, striving to compose himself.

"You will now have to take responsibility," she continued. "You must start to rebuild. This is where you will be proactive in the development of the person you are going to become. A complete transformation of your former self. You have come to a point in your life where your subconscious is saying you cannot continue with the same thought process. It will not allow that anymore. The manifestations are the release of blocked emotions."

Derek looked down at the crumpled tissue in his hands. Rebuild? Where would he even start?

"Remember, forgiveness of others is essential to the healing process," Dr. Cole said. "It will help you to establish mental peace and reestablish good bodily health."

He wondered how that would work when seeing his own appearance caused him literal physical pain.

"When you continue to feel resentment because you have been hurt, mistreated, injured, or deceived, these feelings create inflamed and festering wounds. There is only one way to heal—and that is to perform your own surgery on all these negative feelings. Discard them through forgiveness, one by one." She paused. "Are you willing to forgive, starting with yourself?"

The trauma of being covered head to toe in strange imagery had consumed his every waking moment. "Tell you the truth, I'm not quite sure," Derek admitted.

Dr. Cole stood and hung her suit jacket on the back of the chair. "I would like to make something clear. Just because you forgive someone doesn't mean that you must like that person or associate with them. What forgiveness means is that that you don't wish them any ill will. That you wish for them the same that you wish for anyone. Good health, peace, happiness, and all the blessings of life."

She sat back down. "Remember, this is really a selfish prospect because when you wish well for someone else you are wishing it for yourself. You know the saying, *do unto others*. When you understand the creative law of your own mind, you will cease to blame others and the conditions for which these events took place. Your thoughts create your misery or your happiness."

Derek could still feel the pangs of insecurity caused by people who shot him looks of revulsion and spoke unkind words. It felt like an open wound.

"Let me give you an example," she offered. "Think about electricity. You can use it to kill someone, or you can use it to light a house. The force of the electricity can be used for good or for evil. How you choose to use it is up to you.

"This is the same for how you conduct your thought process. Either choose to look at the positive side and continue to take control of your destiny in a positive manner, or think in a negative way and suffer the consequences. This process is controlled totally by you."

Derek rubbed his forehead. "You make it sound so easy. But my self-esteem hit rock bottom. I've felt like a target, a second-class citizen. I don't feel like my future holds my dreams, hopes, or success anymore. So when it comes to my everyday life, it's more complicated." He thought about the chain that had disappeared off his ankle. He couldn't even make a firm decision about whether it had been a positive development.

"It's only complicated if you view this as a curse or chronic illness," she suggested. "You must decide that no matter what happens, you will stick to a set of rules in your life, a code that you live by."

"I'll never be happy because of these tattoos," he protested. "It's gut-wrenching. It's maddening and isolating!"

"The desire for order, acceptance, and vengeance is why people turn to religion. You are going to have to find something beyond yourself to reach out to in those times when you are feeling low or weak or just alone."

"I do have Kendal now," Derek said, idly touching his chest where her hand had lain.

"It's critical to have someone you can count on," Dr. Cole affirmed. "But that person shouldn't be burdened to carry you every time you feel weak or downcast. There are times when prayer or mediation is necessary to tap into your higher self. You must be able to take care of yourself spiritually. Contribute and be seen as an asset to the relationship. This way the relationship can be nurtured by both people, and it can thrive and grow."

A wave of insecurity flashed over him. "I guess I still have a lot to think about."

She smiled. "You must create new habits. The automatic instinct of what to do in surgery or how to ride your motorcycle—that's the subconscious taking over the decision-making process. This is your second nature. You have the power to choose a good or bad habit. You also have the power to choose a positive or negative thought. We are all under the compulsion of habits. But ultimately you have the power and control over the thought that turns into habit."

"How long do you think this healing process is going to take?" He looked at her pensively.

Dr. Cole shrugged. "How much time and energy are you willing to put into this?"

"Whatever it takes." He squared his shoulders. "Are you sure this will work?"

"I'm sure that no matter what happens you must do this for your survival. Be specific about what you want your life to look like. Then start making that life a reality by living it as if it has already happened."

He raised his eyebrows. "Okay, Doc. I'll do my best."

"You must see it in your mind's eye first." She leaned forward across her desk. "Imagine what you want as vividly as possible, as if it's happening in the moment. Be aware of your feelings as you visualize the specific scenario you wish to play out."

Derek tried to imagine what it would feel like to have the extraordinary capacity to create a new reality.

"For instance, imagine you were to wake up and all the illustrations on your body were to have dissolved. Focus on the positive emotions acquired for your new healthy, normal skin. With practice you can start to exert control over these positive emotions and to manifest a happy and fulfilling life. The changes will happen first emotionally and psychologically, then physically.

"The intelligence within you will take over and immediately start to repair the damage. You can learn to rebuild using positive new emotions that will form fresh impressions on your mind. These impressions in turn can become manifestations."

Derek nodded. "I think I understand."

"Good. Do these exercises at night right before you go to sleep, when your mind is most impressionable. Enter a drowsy state, then convey your messages or images to your subconscious. You should replicate the positive image or message repeatedly. In this state, the negative thoughts are neutralized, and the subconscious is in a state of acceptance."

Derek sat forward in his chair, suddenly remembering something important. "Last night, right before I went to sleep, I was thinking back to when my grandmother read Bible stories to me. I was able to sleep without nightmares for the first time."

Dr. Cole gave him an encouraging nod. "That's a wonderful experience for you to understand the power your imagination and words have on your subconscious. It speaks to you through visualization, attaching the emotion and affirmations. You must understand and believe your visualization according to the feeling and faith behind the conviction."

Derek met her gaze. "You're making sense," he said.

"There's an emotional intelligence that will take care of your body. The difficulty will be the conscious mind. It always tries to interfere because of its five senses. When fears, opinions, and false beliefs are registered, emotional conditioning happens—in your case with drastic results."

Derek looked down sadly at his ink-covered hands.

"Your subconscious works best at night. It's a silent process. It has a life of its own, seeking expression through you. That is why it's so important for you to think correctly because every thought process or action which is not harmonious, whether through ignorance or design, will eventually result in discord and loss."

Derek suppressed a bitter laugh. Yes, he'd lost a great deal. Everything he'd once held dear. But they were mostly material things, he realized. Money, prestige, a luxury penthouse no one ever visited except for his maid. With Kendal . . . well, maybe he'd gotten what he *needed.*

"You'll start to see results in the next few months," Dr. Cole promised. "You build a new body every eleven months. If you build these defects back into your body, these fears, and this anger, you will have no one to blame but yourself."

You are what you think about, Derek told himself.

Dr. Cole rose and put her blazer back on. "You *can* keep from entertaining negative thoughts. Every time the old fear or anger tries to come back, make sure you have a positive replacement thought or image. This will be your conscious exercise for the immediate future. But then it will become automatic, and the changes will be permanent."

She smoothed down the front of her suit. "It is abnormal for you to be sick, fearful, or angry. Healthier conditions can be restored with greater ease and certainty with practice. It took you a lifetime to build this condition. It will certainly take some time to reverse it."

The doctor squeezed around the corner of her desk and opened the door. "Abigail, please make an appointment for Dr.

Hollinger for next week." Her hand rested on the doorknob. "Does that work for you?"

Derek regarded her. "So it could take almost a *year* for the tattoos to disappear?"

"If they disappear at all. What I am saying is that you build a new body every eleven months. You can change your body by changing your thoughts. Just so you know, the principal reason for failure is usually a lack of confidence."

She stepped forward and rested her hand on his shoulder. "When your subconscious mind accepts an idea, it immediately begins to execute it. If you think things are getting worse or taking too long and you start to think things like, 'I will never get the answer' or 'It's hopeless'—well, your subconscious is going to cooperate."

She lifted her hand. "Make sure you go home and relax. Use your imagination and your willpower. Picture yourself without the illustrations. Believe it has already happened. Watch them as they dissolve on each part of your body. Believe it to a point of conviction. Then relax and let it happen."

Derek slowly stood to leave. "I'll do my best."

Outside, Derek straddled his motorcycle and pulled out his cell phone to check for messages. There were none.

Kendal must be busy, he thought. He put his helmet on and shifted the bike into gear.

The more time he spent on his motorcycle, the more he was beginning to feel like another person. Stronger, happier, and more honest. The speed of the bike and rush of adrenaline felt exhilarating. Derek's confidence surged as he leaned into the swerves and corners. An old adage came to mind.

The solution lies within the problem, and the answer is found within the question.

Chapter 17

Derek pulled up in front of Terry's tattoo shop and slowly backstepped his bike into a parking spot until the back wheel came to rest at the curb. He watched as a group of kids walked past carrying surfboards, laughing and joking.

They reminded him of the friends he had as a kid before his world came crashing down. When the boys finally strolled out of sight, Derek climbed off his motorcycle and went into the dark little tattoo shop. The door buzzer rang.

Terry stepped out from behind the beads. "Hey, buddy. What's going on?"

Derek shook his hand. "I came over to see if you can help me answer some more questions. You've already given me a lot of information and I really appreciate it . . . but I hoped you might look at my tattoos up close. See if you can give me any insights about what they mean."

Terry nodded. "Sure, have a seat. Let's see what you got going on." He locked the front door, then perched on a little swivel stool next to Derek. "So, what are we looking at here?"

Derek took off his leather coat. "Well let's start with this one." He pushed up his right sleeve and showed him the shield on his upper right arm. It had two swords crossed above it with a dagger through the middle. "What do you think this means?"

Terry frowned. "Well, the shield and swords symbol come from ancient Sparta. It has to do with being a warrior or victory in a battle. Or it can mean the protector, so it could have to do with being a defender of something . . . or someone. Then the last thing I can think of is the sword with the shield has to do with justice. So, maybe, justice in a battle, something like that. Adding the dagger to it may mean that a trust was broken. So that could mean that a battle was lost because a trust was broken. Or you defended someone and then your trust was broken."

Derek thought about the doctor saying that the tattoos were like a shield to protect against all the hurt. His finger moved over to the jaguar on the inner arm.

"The jaguar represents power. It's the embodiment of aggressiveness." Terry rolled back in his swivel stool.

Derek lifted his shirt. There was hardly an inch of bare skin. Each tattoo was connected to the others by a geometric pattern.

"Those symbols are tied to spiritual and religious practices in ancient times," Terry explained. His brow rose a fraction as he focused on the heart. "It's the inner part of a person, the home of the spirit. It's the core of a person, the place where wisdom is deposited, and, if you're a Christian, where the Lord dwells. A heart can be a symbol of love, but a black heart means heartbreak. Then you have the rose wrapped around it. The black rose means death, whereas the symbol of the rose itself means hope, joy, love, beauty, and Jesus."

Derek pointed to the right side of his chest where a large dark blue dragon wrapped from his side up around the pectoral muscle. "How about that?"

"The dragon has a lot of different meanings," Terry explained, "depending how you view the mythical creature. In general, most guys look at it as representing strength, courage, wisdom, power, and force. Some people use the dragon tattoo to represent themselves as a guardian, especially over loved ones, so they view it as a symbol of protection." He hesitated. "It also represents the Devil."

"That's reassuring," Derek said dryly. He lifted his left arm to reveal a black snake that wrapped around to the back side of the shoulder, where the head and tail came together.

"The serpent or snake can mean wisdom." Terry thought for a moment. "But your serpent is black and eating its own tail. That means death, then eternal return, or cycles that start anew as soon as they end. It can also mean having no ego. The death of an ego."

"No ego?" Derek echoed.

"Like when you were first born." Terry rolled back on the stool. "Before you started learning about things and became conditioned to the environment or you know . . . became tarnished by the world."

Terry rolled closer to study the skull on Derek's right ribcage that wrapped around to his back. "The skull represents change, but most people connect it with fear and danger."

Derek pointed to the black and red spider on his neck. Its spindly legs wrapped around the base of his skull.

"The black and red spider has to do with wisdom, or it can represent an incarceration or capture. A long-legged spider may mean a longstanding issue. Or it could be related to someone who casts spells, or an evil spirit, death, or danger."

Derek felt a prickle of electricity run through his body. "Like a shaman?"

"Yep. Or again it could be a combination of meanings. Like you're captured by your fate. Something like that."

Derek touched the left side of his face. "And this one?"

"Yeah, okay. The teardrop with a dollar sign means that all you can see is money. Grief, trouble, pain caused by money." Terry grimaced. "Sorry, buddy. A lot of this isn't sounding very good."

"No, but I still need to hear it." Derek pointed to his left shoulder blade, where a dog howled at the moon.

"Spiritually, it means you are an unbeliever. It can also signify the encouragement and support you need to overcome the shadows in your life. On the flip side, you have a guardian angel sitting on your shoulder."

"Thanks man," Derek said. "This is all been really helpful."

"Glad to be of service." Terry tapped his shoulder. "The full moon symbolizes time cycles. When the moon becomes full, the boundaries between reality and spirituality are the weakest. The howling of the dog represents strength, free spiritedness, and a connection to the wild."

Derek cleared his throat and patted one thigh. "Uh, you mind if I . . .?"

Terry chuckled . "Sure, go ahead."

He unzipped his pants and lowered them to expose a tree on his thigh.

"Okay, trees are essential to human survival. Because it's showing its roots, it can mean a connection to the past. When you have the roots, it symbolizes nourishment. The roots also anchor it down and keep it secure through times of trouble or hardship. It can be a warning of judgement."

Around his right knee a trail of stars connected to another trail of stars.

"Stars have to do with excellence or nobility," Terry said. "For early sailors it was how they found their way home. People are said to look to the stars as a way of self-guidance. Believers look at them as angels."

"Angels," Derek repeated softly. His head spun with new revelations, new meanings. "Okay, look at these three guys on my back. What do you think about them?"

He pulled his pants up and turned around.

"These faces should have a direct meaning for *you*," Terry said in a level tone. "When you have someone's face inked on your body, it's usually some type of memorial. A special relationship or a relationship lost." He frowned. "These guys don't look too friendly. Where do they come from?"

Derek sighed. There was no point in hiding it. His body was an open book—literally. "I'm pretty sure those are the guys who tried to kill me when I was young."

Terry looked taken aback. "Seriously, man? Wow, that sucks. And now you got 'em inked on your back?"

"That's the main reason why I came to see you. I was hoping you could help me answer that question. Why are they all sitting in the middle of the spider's web?"

Terry chewed his lip thoughtfully. "Well, here's something you might like, bro. The spider web represents a lengthy term in prison. It's a predator's trap. In prison it can have many different meanings. I think it's individualistic to the wearer. But generally, you want to watch your back from people like this."

Derek tugged his shirt on, a bitter taste in his mouth. "Yeah, well, too late."

"I noticed you have the number twenty-one tatted on the side of your scalp. I haven't seen that one before." Terry gave him a sympathetic look. "Maybe these tattoos have some significance about the future, not just the past. The way all your tattoos are linked with a geometric design tells me maybe you got some unfinished business, my friend."

"Maybe." Derek zipped up his leather jacket. "I don't know what that would be, but I hope to heck I figure it out soon."

He held out a hand. Terry shook it. "Thanks a lot, buddy, you've given me a lot to think about. What do I owe you?"

Terry pointed to his left eye. "Nothing, brother."

Derek understood he was pointing out the teardrop with a dollar sign and reminding him that there was more to life than money.

"Thanks again. You have my card. Don't hesitate, okay? If I can ever help you out with anything, just give me a call."

"I'll keep that in mind, Doc."

Terry walked him to the door and unlocked it. A young man entered. He rubber-necked as Derek walked out. "Whoa, man, sick. That's what I want to do."

Derek turned and saw the kid staring with admiration. "Yeah, sick," he muttered, turning away. "That sums it up perfectly."

Chapter 18

When Derek arrived back at the apartment, he found Kendal working away in the kitchen. "Hey, what's up?" he called.

Kendal turned to him. She wore a pair of shorts and halter top that definitely improved the view. "It's barbeque night." she proclaimed. "I bought two steaks. Please tell me you like steak."

He smiled. "I like steak."

She beamed back at him. "I have a couple of potatoes in the microwave, and I thought we could have some asparagus with it. How does that sound?"

He felt the urge to pull her into his arms and kiss her soft lips, but he wasn't sure exactly where they stood. "Ah, perfect," he stammered.

"I still have a bottle of red wine in the cabinet if you could take it out and open it. The glasses are right above." Kendal went back to seasoning the meat.

Derek checked the labels, found a red, and started rooting through the upper shelves for the wine glasses. "You keep a pretty classy bar here," he teased.

"Hey, don't complain." She shot him a look of mock reproach over one shoulder. "We have everything we need."

"Yes, we do." Derek agreed, studying the curves of her back and the way her hair brushed her shoulders.

"Come on." Kendal backed him out of the tiny kitchen. "I want to get to the barbeque first or we could be waiting half the night. Bring the wine," she called, then disappeared out the front door.

He picked up the glasses and wine bottle off the counter then joined Kendal at the grill where a middle-aged man he'd never seen before was flipping burgers.

"We're up next," she said. "Roy, this is Derek."

Roy looked up, raised an eyebrow, and gave a nod.

"Hey," Derek said, feeling more than a little awkward.

"Since we're going to be here for a while, do me a favor and run up and get our chairs from the deck," Kendal said.

"Sure." He turned to go.

"What's up?" Roy asked her. "Is that your new boyfriend?"

Derek could overhear them as he walked away.

"No. Just a friend."

Derek winced slightly. Well, he'd said as much about her to the psychologist. But he wasn't kidding himself anymore. Now he did want more from her. *Take it slow*, he thought. *Don't rush her. Especially with all the crazy you've brought into her world.*

"Is he staying with you?" Roy persisted, his voice carrying across the courtyard.

Busybody, Derek thought, pausing to listen as he entered the door of the apartment.

"He has his own place. He just . . . has a couple of things he needs to sort out."

"What's up with all the tats?"

"Oh, that's a very long story. But he's really a nice guy. He's a doctor."

Derek smiled to himself. He liked being described that way—and hoped she meant it.

"No kidding." Roy sounded doubtful.

Derek returned with the chairs and held one out for Kendal. He'd show this guy that he could be chivalrous.

"Thanks." Kendal sat. "So . . . you're buying?" She grinned and looked over at the bottle of wine he'd left on the wall.

"You bet I am." He'd just picked it up and located the corkscrew when a tall, slim bald man and a small, cute brunette approached.

Kendal called out a greeting. "Hi, Mark, hi, Karen!"

"How are you?" Karen replied with a smile.

"Great." Kendal hugged Karen first, then Mark. "I want you to meet my friend Derek." Kendal motioned at Derek, who was still struggling to get the cork out of the bottle.

Derek stepped forward to shake Mark's hand. He was reaching for Karen's hand when she flinched and moved behind her husband. Mark was obviously embarrassed by his wife's behavior. So was Derek, until Kendal slid her arm through his. He gave her a grateful smile.

"We're having steak tonight," she said, unflustered by Karen's rudeness. "What are you two planning to barbeque?"

Mark quickly explained that they had only come over to say hello and wouldn't be staying. They were heading out to dinner.

"That's too bad," Kendal said. "We're just about to have some wine." She smiled into Derek's eyes. He felt a warm flutter low in his stomach. Suddenly, he was glad her friends weren't sticking around.

"I'm all done," Roy yelled from the barbeque. "NEXT!"

"Well, that's us." Kendal cheerfully turned with Derek still locked in her arm to claim their turn at the barbeque. She put the steaks on the grill while he pulled the cork and poured the wine.

"Here you go," he said, handing her the glass.

"Cheers." Kendal clicked her glass against his.

He glanced at the departing couple. "Listen, I'm so sorry about that."

"Please! You have nothing to be sorry for."

"Yeah, I do. I'm at your home, around your friends, and I'm making it uncomfortable for you."

She sipped her wine and arched a brow. "I'm not uncomfortable."

"Well, they certainly are."

Kendal smiled, "I guess they are not the friends I thought they were. Cheers."

"So . . . you know how to barbeque?"

"Yes. What about you? Do you know how to barbeque?"

Derek shrugged with a smirk.

"I thought not. You can reconstruct someone's whole body, but you have no clue how to cook a steak, do you?"

"Nope, but I bet you could teach me."

Kendal handed him the tongs. "I'll tell you when they're ready to turn. You'd better listen." She grinned. "This is our dinner we are talking about here."

"Yes, ma'am."

Kendal moved closer and took a sip of wine. "Just making sure you don't mess up my steak."

"Oh, I see." He nodded seriously. "It's all about the steak."

"Yes, and after you turn the steaks, remember you have to put the asparagus on the grill."

"Wow, I am really getting the full cooking class tonight."

"You bet you are. You have to learn to feed yourself at some point."

"You mean as opposed to having other people feed me?" He chuckled.

"Exactly," Kendal agreed.

The sun had gone down and the temperature was rapidly dropping.

"Oh, my goodness, I'm getting really cold." She shivered. "I think I had better go up and get my jacket."

"I can keep you warm. Come here." He wrapped his arms around her. "Is this a little better?"

"Much," she clasped his arms and they stood for a minute, sharing each other's warmth. He wished they could stay like that forever, just the two of them. How far he had come from his old hectic, workaholic life. It felt good, even though the future was still so uncertain.

"What do you think will happen to my practice?" Derek asked after a minute.

"You'll go back to your office and run it like you always have," Kendal said firmly.

"I appreciate the vote of confidence, but I'm talking seriously now."

She half turned to him. "You know what? You'll figure it out."

"I guess I'll have to at some point." He eyed the grill.

"Yeah, you will, but not tonight." She smiled. "Right now, you need to turn those steaks and put the asparagus on."

A few minutes later, they climbed the stairs with dinner in

hand. Kendal grabbed some napkins as Derek headed straight out to the patio deck to put the chairs back.

"Do you need anything for your steak?" she called from the kitchen.

"No, I'm good!"

She took the potatoes out of the microwave, put them on a plate, then took the butter out of the refrigerator and turned just in time to hand them to Derek who carried it all out to the deck. With forks and steak knives in hand, Kendal followed. They both managed to organize their plates and sit down at the same time.

Derek topped off their wine glasses. "This is really nice," he said.

"Yeah, it is," Kendal agreed.

He took a bite of his steak. "And man, am I a good cook."

Kendal grinned. "Yes, you are. My hat goes off to the chef. Not bad for a rookie."

He poked his fork at her with a mock scowl. "Who are you calling a rookie?"

Kendal laughed. "Listen, I have to be in San Diego tomorrow."

"What's going on in San Diego?"

"I volunteer with an organization to help the homeless. They have this big event once a year where they bring professionals together to offer their services."

How little he knew about her, Derek reflected. But he wasn't surprised. Kendal had a big heart. "What time do you have to be there?"

"Very early." She took a bite of potato. "It starts right after daybreak. Would you like to go with me?"

"Sure. I've never done anything like that. Do I have to tell them who I am?"

"If you want to volunteer as a doctor, then yes."

He hesitated. "What if I just volunteer as a medical assistant, but not as a doctor?"

"You can do that, too."

"I think it might be smarter not to have them asking a bunch of questions, don't you think?"

She nodded. "Keeping a low profile is probably best."

Derek found he was looking forward to it. "You want to take the motorcycle? It's a great ride down to San Diego along the coast."

She hesitated. "I've never taken a long ride on a motorcycle before. You know, a real road trip."

"You'll love it," he promised. "It's like flying. Even better than zipping around in your car with the top down. You're going to have a great time."

Kendal leaned back in her chair, resting her feet up on Derek's lap. He took her sandals off and started to massage her feet. "How often do you volunteer for the homeless?"

She sighed happily as he dug into her arches. "Ah, this one tomorrow? I went last year, so this will be the second time."

"Do you volunteer other places?" he asked, fingers moving up her calf.

"Yes. I volunteer at the homeless shelter at the beach. I try . . . oh darn, that feels so good. I try to go over there once or twice a month to help when I can."

Derek pulled her legs so that her feet were wrapped around

him and started to rub her thighs.

"You're pretty good at this," she said softly.

"I am?" He teased. "You don't think I need lessons?"

She gazed at him with a spark of heat. "Would you like me to give you lessons?"

How beautiful she looked. His heart beat faster. "Well, you've been a pretty good teacher so far," he whispered. Derek leaned forward and gave Kendal a deep, passionate kiss. He felt her body respond. Her fingers stroked the back of his neck.

"My room," she whispered.

He kissed her again, inhaling the sweet smell of her hair. Then he lifted her up and carried her into the bedroom.

An hour later, they snuggled together, Kendal lazily running her finger over the lines of the tattoos on Derek's chest. Suddenly, he felt her stiffen.

"Derek," she whispered. "My God, the heart has changed color. Look!"

He opened his eyes and glanced down. What used to be a big black heart with thorny black roses twined around it was now a bright red heart with colorful blooms and green vines.

"Whoa," he muttered. "That's pretty wild."

He knew for sure now that this was no bizarre prank. It was supernatural. Metaphysical. Something beyond rational understanding. And it was changing. *Evolving.* Just as Dr. Cole had predicted.

"What does it mean?" Kendal wondered.

"I don't know." He sat up in bed, letting the sheet fall away. "Tell me if you see any other changes."

Kendal began to explore the rest of Derek's body, examining each illustration.

"Huh," she said at last. "I don't see anything new. Though there could be some subtle alterations, I just didn't notice them." She rubbed his back with a smile. "I don't have them all memorized yet."

He gave her a soft kiss. "Okay, but do me a favor and check my back. Is the big one with the faces still there?"

She examined his back. "Yep. They all look the same."

His jaw clenched. The changing heart felt like a good sign, but the childhood attack was one of his primal traumas. Until he dealt with that, he suspected none of the rest of it could be truly resolved. "Damn it," he muttered.

"Well, let's just think about it a second. When was the last time you saw the black heart?"

"When I took off my shirt, right before we climbed into bed. I think I saw it when I glanced in the mirror."

She arched a brow. "You glanced in the mirror when we were making love?"

He laughed. "No. That's not what I meant. It was just a glimpse. And honestly, Kendal, every time I see myself in the mirror, I still can't believe it's me."

She regarded him with that open, direct look he'd grown to adore. "Do you think our lovemaking had anything to do with the change?"

"It sure seems like it, doesn't it? But I wonder how that would work. I mean how could it have changed the tattoo?"

"If they're a projection of your subconscious mind, like Dr. Cole claims, maybe it could be connected to an act or a certain emotion? Or I don't know . . . chemicals secreted in your body?" She laughed. "No, that sounds weird. But you have to admit, it's all pretty nuts."

"I don't deny it," he said dryly. "Terry said the black heart means that either I'm heartless, or I had my heart broken by someone. Or by a tragic event." He held her eyes. "Maybe this means I'm starting to get my heart back again."

"So, what does the red heart mean?"

"Well, it represents love. And a heart with wings symbolizes a person with a joyful and free spirit." He gave her a crooked grin. "Though we both know that's not me."

She poked his ribs. "No, I don't know that. You've been through a lot in your life. It's understandable that you're a serious person." She touched his chest. "Anyway, *your* heart has a vine and rose around it, not wings."

"I did notice that the chains around my ankles are gone. I haven't had those for a while."

"What? When did that happen?" Kendal pulled down the sheets.

He glanced away. "I didn't say anything, but I think it happened the night we went out to the beach."

"Why didn't you tell me, Derek?" She looked hurt. "This is important."

He met her eyes. "I think my insecurities got in the way. I was struggling about where our relationship was going. I didn't notice the chain was gone until we got home that night, and it was after you had already gone to bed."

"You mean the night of your bar fight?"

"The night we first kissed." He touched her cheek. "I could feel a change then, too, Kendal. There was so much that happened that night. I wasn't sure it was connected to the kiss until now. I didn't want to get my hopes up—or yours." His brow furrowed. "I wonder if the rest of the tattoos are going to change?"

She cupped his cheek with a smile. "I think that if one of them changed, then all of them could change, or even disappear like the chain from your ankle."

He nodded slowly. "Well, one thing we do know is right before we made love, the heart was black. And after, it was red. So I'd say it's based on emotion."

She studied his face. Her mouth curled in a smile, but her gaze was serious. "Are you saying you have feelings for me?"

"Yes." He pulled her to his chest, holding her tight. "That's the only thing that's changed. How I feel about you." He let out a long exhale, stroking her hair. "Maybe there is something to this. This is what the doctor was telling me.

"She said I may have some sort of control subconsciously over these markings. That somehow these markings *are* a reaction by my subconscious or spirit brought on when the woman put the curse on me. I think subconsciously, I responded to her words— even though I don't remember what those words were. I can tell you one thing, they were nothing good. She was not wishing me well. That's for sure."

He stared up at the ceiling. "I think subconsciously I

responded to whatever hex or curse she put on me out of fear. Now it appears I have some sort of conscious or subconscious way to change or hopefully reverse it."

"Oh, Derek, I hope so," she said with feeling. "That would be wonderful. I know how much this has torn your world apart."

"Well, it *has* made me realize some things. I've depended way too much on my practice for fulfillment. I haven't had any personal relationships or built any friendships over the years. I didn't speak to my mother before she passed away and I don't have any other family. I basically don't have anyone except the people I know in business, my partners, and you. I spent all my time building the practice. And when I had a crisis, there was no one to turn to. It made me realize that I haven't built anything solid."

Derek kissed Kendal on the top of her head. "But I'm ready to make a change. I think that starts with you. I know there's a lot I need to figure out. But knowing I have someone who cares about me will make the fight that much more worthwhile."

She tipped her face up, kissing him back. "I'm here for you, whatever you need. But let's get some sleep. We have a big day ahead of us."

"It's going to be a beautiful ride down the coast tomorrow. We can leave a little earlier, stop for breakfast and watch the sun come up."

"I would love that," she murmured.

"Well, you are in for a treat." He switched off the bedside lamp.

"Now I'm starting to get excited," she said with a giggle. "It's going to be hard to get to sleep."

He nuzzled her neck. "Let me prescribe something that will help."

Derek rolled Kendal to her back and started kissing her again, slow and deep. He wanted her to feel all the intensity of his own emotions. He wanted her to feel the passion beating in his new rose-colored heart.

Chapter 19

The week had taken its toll, leaving their pent-up feelings ready for release. A night of lovemaking left them exhilarated. Derek and Kendal were on the road before daybreak.

A quick breakfast at a cozy diner left her relaxed and content. It felt familiar, yet new and exciting at the same time. By the time they arrived in San Diego the bright morning sun beat down on a line of homeless people that wound along the street for as far as the eye could see.

Derek rode up to the front gate of the tent city. The security guard checked Kendal's pass card and waved them through. Derek found a place to park off to the side on the grass.

"Those are the volunteers." Kendal took off her helmet and pointed to the row of massive tents. She unzipped her backpack and found a piece of paper. "Looks like we continue down to the end of the row. We should see the tent we'll be working in."

Derek pulled his cap out of his side saddle. "Lead the way." He kept his tone light, but walking down the row of tents, he started feeling nervous about the reception he would receive.

"This one is for people to clean up any type of misdemeanor violations," she said as they passed the first tent. "There's court staff and judges who volunteered to come in for the day. Next is the dental care tent. If the treatment can't be finished in one visit, the staff might set up some type of ongoing assistance to help the person get back to a healthy state."

She pointed. "Over there are the showers and fresh clothes. Then hairdressers who give cuts and shaves, things like that. The next tent is for job seekers. Volunteers help people fill out the applications and give them a way to stay in contact with potential employers."

They walked along the row. There was a spiritual tent for various religious denominations, which took turns throughout the day. Across the way, he saw a sign for therapists and psychologists.

"They help get people off the street," Kendal explained. "Possibly by placing them in a group home or hospital, or by trying to contact relatives." She steered him to another large tent. "This is us. I do a basic physical. If they should have any injury, we treat it. If they have symptoms of disease, then we connect them to the right welfare agency to get them the help that they need."

Derek nodded. "Perfect. I'll follow your lead."

Upon entering the tent, they were given name tags. Kendal introduced Derek as her assistant, which seemed to tickle her judging by the amused smile on her lips.

As they walked deeper into the tent, he whispered, "Don't get too used to this. It's not going to be long before you're assisting me again."

"We'll see," she laughed.

"Hey," Derek objected teasingly.

Kendal gave him a quick kiss and grabbed an armful of medical supplies off the table.

Multiple beds sat row after row. Equipment lined the walls of the tent, creating a portable field hospital. It made for a convenient treatment center that would provide paramedic-style attention, without overburdening hospital emergency rooms.

"This place looks like a M.A.S.H. unit," he said softly, looking around the massive tent. A whistle blew. "What does that mean?" Derek asked.

"They're opening the gates. Get ready."

For the next several hours, they administered medical care to an endless multitude. It was like being dropped into a disaster zone. They treated people suffering from poor nutrition, drug abuse, chronic illnesses like diabetes and heart disease . . . the list went on.

Derek looked around as he finished with his last patient. A logistical difficulty had been tackled wisely, he thought. The idea to bring the sick and disabled to mobile medical facilities was ingenious. Kendal was still busy, so he signaled to her that he was going to take a break. She gave an absent nod as she checked the vitals of an older man in ragged, second-hand clothing.

Derek cleaned his hands with sanitizer and walked out of the medical tent. The time had passed swiftly. From the angle of the sun, it must be late afternoon already. He followed the sound of music to the spiritual tent. A preacher dressed in a black shirt, white clerical collar, and dark pants stood on stage talking to a group of people. Curious, Derek moved closer to listen.

"There is a passage in the Bible that speaks of faith as a shield against the curse and against the influence of the Devil," the preacher bellowed. "Faith means to trust in the LORD. The best way to get rid of a curse is to have a union with GOD."

He marched across the front of the stage. "What I tell you is true! Curses are the work of the Devil and the only way you can counter a curse is by spiritual means. By having a constant relationship with GOD."

The man stopped and surveyed the crowd. "I know there is someone here today that has been sent specifically to hear this message. Now, you are the best person to determine what this means to you."

He jumped down and put his hand on a man sitting in the front row with his head hanging low. "I know what this means to me, it means having a relationship with God through the HOLY SPIRIT, the source above all spirits. What does it mean to you?"

People shook their heads or nodded. Others just seemed transfixed by the preacher's intensity.

"There will come a time when that sinful spirit can't curse you anymore," his voice thundered. "That wicked spirit will see GOD himself in you. It will be afraid of YOU! This will happen when you become united with GOD. If you are already a victim of a curse, suffering, you can be saved by repenting. Take the power back with GOD'S glory."

Intrigued by the word "curse", Derek sat down in one of the folding chairs.

The preacher's voice softened. "If you love the Lord, give Him praise. Then listen, you will hear the voice of the Lord come from your heart." He hugged a Bible to his chest, then raised it in the air. "Only He can set you free. Repent and ask forgiveness for what you have done.

"You might be told to pay restitution to the person you have wronged, or He may ask that you forgive those who have wronged you. Only then can you be released from the curse. Repair the damage that has been done!"

He stopped to make eye contact with someone in the front row. "I want to remind you that your strength must come from your faith in the Lord's mighty power. Wear all of God's armor so that you will be able to stand safe against all the strategies and tricks that Satan will devise against you."

He raised both hands out to the crowd. "For we are not fighting against people made of flesh and blood, but against demons without bodies, the evil rulers of the unseen world, those mighty satanic beings and great evil princes. Against huge numbers of wicked spirits in the spirit world and all evildoers who rule here on earth."

He turned slowly and went back to the pulpit in the middle of the stage, setting his Bible down on top of it. He lowered his mouth to the microphone. "Know the Spirit of God. Every person that accepts Jesus Christ into their heart belongs to God. So use every piece of God's armor to resist the enemy, to repent! Read your Bible, pray, and love your neighbor. When the evil one attacks, he will have no authority over you while you stand with Our Lord and Savior, Jesus Christ."

Standing with his legs apart, his jaw firm, he proclaimed, "To do this you must wear the strong belt of Truth which is given in the scripture." His face softened. "Let us love one another because *God is love.*"

He raised the Bible up. "In every battle, faith is your shield and love is your ammunition. To stop the fiery arrows aimed at your

Helmet of Redemption, you must have confidence in God and do as He has asked. The Sword of the Spirit which is the Word of God will be your salvation.

"Pray and read your Bible!" He shook the book in the air. "This is how we know that we remain in Him, and He in us. Ask God for all that is in line with the Holy Spirit's wishes."

The preacher held the Bible out in front between his praying hands. "Plead with him, reminding him of your needs, and keep praying earnestly for all Christians everywhere. We know that we belong to God, and the whole world is under the power of the evil one. We also know that the son of God gave us the Holy Spirit which gives us the discernment to know the one who is true."

He looked up. "Pray for me, too, that God's hand is upon me to offer the right words as I eagerly tell others about the Lord. Amen."

The crowd repeated, "Amen, Amen."

Just as the sermon ended, one of the men stood up and turned. Derek's breath hitched. He moved closer. The preacher stood talking inside a circle of men. Derek heard a loud laugh. A laugh he could never forget. That made his skin crawl and his chest tighten until he could hardly breathe.

The Devil's laugh.

For a moment, he was that broken little boy again. Derek nearly ran from the tent, jumped on his bike, and gunned it out of there. But he thought of Kendal, just across the way in the medical tent, and it gave him strength. What would she tell him to do?

Derek drew a deep breath. All his life, he'd been running from this man. From the terror and helplessness. But he wouldn't run anymore. He pushed his way into the circle, temples pounding. There, standing in the middle, was a man with a web across his face and a spider on his cheek. A wave of dizziness hit as he recognized the tat. Derek must have staggered because the preacher took his arm and guided him to one of the folding chairs.

Derek forced himself to take another, closer look at the guy who had assaulted him all those years ago. He was a frail old man now. When he threw his head back to laugh, Derek glimpsed a toothless black hole. The man's eyes were yellow. He weighed all of a hundred pounds.

Both spindly arms were illustrated, down to the tips of his fingers. His neck and head were also completely covered. A devil tattoo marked his neck. It was obvious from the symbolism and lousy quality that most of the tattoos had been done in prison.

The preacher came back with a glass of water. "What can I help you with, son?"

Close up, Derek could see that the preacher wasn't much older than he was. The man had intense blue eyes framed by dark brown hair and a day-old growth of stubble.

"Who's that guy over there with the web on his face?" Derek asked.

The preacher glanced over his shoulder. "His name is Spider. I think it's a childhood nickname. I've tried to get his real name but no luck." He shrugged. "His probation officer would know. Spider was just released from prison."

Derek was not surprised in the least by this bit of news. "What was he in for?"

"A gang fight about twenty-five years ago. He was convicted of murder. They gave him twenty to life, but he got out on good behavior." The preacher sat down next to Derek. "He has hepatitis C and liver cancer. He's dying. By the looks of him, I don't think he could harm anyone."

He's been in prison all this time. Derek stared at the tattoo of a snake that wrapped around his arm and swallowed its own tail.

"Do you know him?" The preacher eyed him curiously.

Derek hesitated. "No, I don't."

"Well, he's not going to be with us much longer. He's very ill. Very frail. He spent his whole adult life in prison and if he doesn't repent, he's going to have to answer for what he's done. I'm looking for his family so he doesn't end up dying alone."

"That's kind of you," Derek muttered, still watching Spider.

The preacher patted his shoulder. "Take care, son. And walk the straight and narrow. You don't want to end up like Spider."

Derek sat for a minute. Then he headed over to the medical tent and watched Kendal treat her patients. What were the odds that the bogeyman from his childhood would be here? Today? That Derek would somehow cross paths with him? Once, he would have scoffed and called it a coincidence, but he knew better now. Fate had turned his life upside down—and fate had brought him here to set things right. Brought them both here.

The fear he had lived with all his life drained away. As a man, he'd pushed it down deep, pretended it didn't exist. Buried himself in work and cut himself off from any relationship that might require honesty. But seeing Spider made him realize that he'd been caught in the past like a fly trapped in amber. The world had moved on. His attacker was a pathetic old man now. Maybe it was time Derek moved on, too.

Spider sauntered out of the spiritual tent, looked around, then pulled a cigarette out of his pocket and lit it. He spat on the ground as Derek approached. "Sorry pal, I only got enough smokes to last me the rest of the day, so I can't be giving any out. You'll have to go bum a butt from someone else."

"You don't recognize me, do you?" Derek asked, amazed at how calm his voice sounded.

How many times had he feared this moment? Had nightmares about the face that stared back at him?

"No. Why should I?" Spider puffed smoke from his nostrils. "From the look of your tats . . . maybe prison?"

Derek stared at him coldly. "I guess you wouldn't, since it took half a dozen operations to put my face back together after you got finished with it."

The ex-con didn't seem bothered at all by this revelation. "No kidding?" He chuckled. "I did that? Wow, you look like you got some dandy work done there."

Derek sorely wanted to punch Spider in the face, but violence would just land him in jail. "Let me refresh your memory. When I was only fourteen, I was walking home from school when you and your thug friends drove up in a car, jumped out, and almost beat me to death."

Spider squinted through a cloud of smoke. "That was you? Damn, I thought you were dead."

"I was in a coma for weeks," he snapped. "It took almost a year before I could walk or talk again."

Spider laughed. "You're one tough son of a gun, aren't you?"

Derek drew a deep, calming breath. Why had he expected even

an iota of remorse? The guy was clearly a psychopath. "All I've ever wanted to know is why on earth you came after me in the first place. I'd never seen any of you before in my life!"

Spider took a drag from the cigarette and shook his head. "Hell, I didn't come after *you*. If I remember right, we were out looking for one of the other gangs in the area that had messed up one of ours just the day before. You were wearing their colors or something. We didn't find out until later that you weren't with a gang. It was all over the papers and on the TV. We thought for sure they were gonna come get us." Another laugh. "But no one ever did."

"I was just an innocent kid walking home from school," Derek exclaimed in disbelief. "There was no way I looked like a gangbanger."

Spider shrugged. "Yeah, probably not, but we were pretty pissed off and we wanted to take it out on someone. I guess you, my friend, were the lucky guy." Spider smiled with his black hole mouth, then spat on the ground.

"I can't believe it was something that stupid," Derek muttered. He realized that some part of him had believed he was at fault somehow. That he'd brought it on himself.

"Yep, they'd messed up one of our guys pretty good and we wanted to get 'em back."

Derek stared at him in disgust. "You're a pathetic human being. If you weren't already half dead—"

"You and a dozen other people," Spider sneered. "Get in line."

Derek unclenched his fists. "No. I'm not going to waste my time." He stabbed a finger at Spider's hollow chest. "You, *my friend*, are on your way to damnation. And you're going to have to answer for what you've done."

"You really think that's how it works?" Spider blustered.

"Yes. I do," Derek said in an even tone. "I think you have a lot of dancing to do in some pretty hot flames."

A bitter expression twisted Spider's sallow features. "This world is where I've been dancing in those hot flames." He took a last drag from the cigarette and crushed the butt under one cheap sneaker. "I think I'm ready to get out of this hellhole. Wherever I'm going can't be much worse."

Derek regarded him without pity. "We make our own destiny. And it sounds like you did a pretty piss-poor job of yours. You spent most of your life in prison. Now that you're out, you're dying from a terminal disease. Sounds like you reaped exactly what you sowed."

"Well, now, don't you sound like the preacher? You should go in and see him. I bet he would be real happy to talk to a sap like you."

"That's probably the best idea you've had," Derek retorted. "I know your life is short. I can't say that I hope that you don't suffer a terrible, slow, gruesome death. But I can try my best to completely put you out of my mind." He turned to leave, then stopped. "Hey, Spider, what happened to the other guys that were with you that day?"

"Ah, they all got knocked off. The last one was shanked in prison about a year or so ago." His chest puffed out, but Derek saw the fear and loneliness in his eyes. "I'm the last one standing."

He left Spider standing outside the tent, lighting another cigarette. Guess he was doing his best to add lung cancer to the list. Derek still felt angry that the man who had nearly ended his life had barely given him another thought, but he also felt lighter. Like he'd shed a burden that he'd carried for so long, he wasn't even aware of it.

Derek found the preacher talking to a couple of people. They walked away as he approached.

"Well, hello there." The preacher smiled. "Welcome back. I was hoping I might see you again."

"Hello, preacher," he said with an answering smile.

"Call me Father Mike."

"Okay, Father Mike. I just had an interesting conversation with Spider." He met the man's mild gaze. "I wasn't truthful before when you asked me if I knew him. Spider and his friends jumped me and left me for dead when I was a kid."

Father Mike grimaced and crossed himself. "I'm sorry, son. How did that go?"

Derek looked away. "Better than I expected. I didn't know what I was going to say or do, but as I stood there with all the anger and hate in me for this man, it just started to dissipate when I realized how he'd wasted his life. He's gotten enough of my energy for one lifetime. It's time to move on. He's not going to be with us much longer, and I really don't want to think about him anymore."

Father Mike nodded sympathetically. "I hope you found some inner peace, son. All things on earth will be taken care of when we pass. That's why it is important for us to do the best we can while we have the opportunity. That man had a demon living in him."

"I believe he *is* the Devil!" Derek said. "Or close enough."

"You may be right. If he isn't, he sure has done a lot of the Devil's work."

"Why is he here?" Derek frowned. "What was he doing in your tent today?"

"He's looking for help from the church to assist him when the time comes. We have a charity group that runs a hospice. Someone he runs around with told him about it."

"Are you going to take care of him?"

"We don't judge people. That's for God to do. We're here to serve. That's it."

The pastor's simple faith and humility touched him. There were good people in the world, too, Derek reminded himself. "Well, God bless you, Padre, I had better get back to work before someone comes looking for me."

Father Mike handed him a pamphlet. "I'll be here all day if you need to talk more, son."

Derek thanked him and returned to the medical tent. He stuffed the brochure into his back pocket as Kendal approached.

"Hey, you," she said with a smile. "Where have you been? I was beginning to wonder if you were coming back."

"I'll tell you about it later. Where do you want me to go?"

She pointed to a line of chairs filled with people who had their shoes off. "They were asking for help over there a few minutes ago. Their shoes don't fit right, and their feet get pretty torn up. You can bandage blisters, try to do some triage."

"Okay, I'm on it." Derek gave Kendal a quick kiss.

He headed over to the waiting patients. They greeted him with smiles. It had been a while since he'd had that kind of reception from anyone but Kendal. Derek smiled back.

For the first time in weeks—years, really—he felt like everything would be okay.

Chapter 20

Exhausted, Derek and Kendal arrived back at the apartment after midnight. Kendal turned on a light and glanced back to see Derek still standing at the front door with his helmet in hand. It was the first good look she'd had of him since they left San Diego.

"Look in the mirror!" Kendal exclaimed.

He turned and stared into the rattan frame.

The tattoo that once covered most of his face had diminished. The smaller tattoos, including the dollar sign on his cheek, were all that remained. Too emotionally drained even to smile, he set his helmet on the table and slowly sat down.

Kendal slipped onto his lap. "Are you okay?"

"I saw the guy who beat me up when I was a kid," he said in a low voice.

She leaned back to study his face. "What? Where?"

"The spiritual tent. I recognized his tattoos."

"Today? What was he doing at the spiritual tent?"

"Looking for hospice care. He's dying of liver cancer from hepatitis C."

She blew out a long breath. "Isn't *that* a shame," she said flatly.

Derek summoned the ghost of a smile. "I basically told him as much."

"You talked to him?" she asked with concern.

"Yes."

Her eyes were wide. "What did you say?"

"I told him I knew he was the guy who almost beat me to death when I was a kid."

"What was his response?"

"He said he was surprised I survived. He thought I was dead."

"Cold," she said softly.

"Yep, no remorse. He's been in prison since right after the beating. He was convicted of the murder of some other guy."

She wrapped her arms around herself. "That's horrible."

"Yeah, and now they released him early because he's dying."

"They should have let him die right there in his jail cell," she said angrily.

"I don't know. Right now, he's out on the street looking for charity, so that can't be too much fun, especially in his condition."

"What happened to the guys that were with him?"

"He said they were all dead."

"What a shocker," she said grimly. "Live by the sword die by the sword. These guys were a pretty violent gang. It all caught up with them."

Derek took her hand. "I guess so."

"So . . ." She studied his face. "How are you feeling about all of this?"

He leaned back, staring up at the ceiling. "Like I just got rid of a big black cloud over my head. I don't know if it was because I didn't know *why* they had done it, or why they had done it *to me*. And the answer is . . . it was random, Kendal. Meaningless. But I survived." He squeezed her hand. "And if it brought us together, I'd do it all over again."

Her eyes shone with unshed tears. "Let's just concentrate on our future."

"You're right. I do want to concentrate on *our* future." He glanced at himself in the hall mirror. "But I'm still not my old self. What if these tattoos never go away?"

She cupped his cheek, turning him to face her. "You know, I was reading some things online about the tattoo culture. Just so you know, the Army relaxed their rules on tattoos. So did a lot of the other branches, including the Coast Guard."

His brows rose. "Are you saying I should join the military?"

"No, silly." She laughed. "I'm saying that the culture is so widespread that even the government is now recognizing they have to lighten up a little on their policies because so many young people, something like 30 percent, have tattoos. Even in visible places like the back of their neck and hands. It's a pretty big policy change."

"I'd never noticed so many people with tattoos before," Derek agreed. "They can be a great way for young people to hide their insecurities and boost their self-esteem."

Kendal looked excited. "I was thinking. What if you started marketing to the Hollywood crowd? There are plenty of people looking to have work removed. And I doubt any of them would object to their doctor being tatted out. In fact, I'm thinking this could actually work for you, Derek!"

"It's definitely worth considering," he agreed dryly, "since my current clientele won't want anything to do with me."

She lightly touched his shoulder. "Yeesh, so gloomy. I doubt people are really that harsh. A lot of the companies that used to have a policy against even showing tattoos are conceding that the new face of the American worker is decorated with ink."

He laughed. "Okay, well I guess you can call me 'The Face of America.'"

Kendal grinned and gave him a kiss. "The companies quoted in the article said they had to compromise because the youth of America are expressing themselves with body art."

"Is that what they call it?"

"I think the reason that most of the companies are relenting is because their workers are college-educated, but it probably depends on the industry. That's why I was thinking that you could go after a target audience. You know, who'd think it was cool to have an illustrated plastic surgeon."

He kissed her neck. "You do, huh?"

Kendal giggled. "The social acceptability of body art has really increased in the past decade."

Derek stroked her knee. "And you know this how?"

"Because I was reading about it online. Practically everyone my age has at least one tattoo." She shrugged. "The more popular it becomes, the more regrets there will be later."

He couldn't help but laugh. "That's true. But why do I still get the negative reactions then, if everyone is so tolerant?"

"Well, you have to admit yours are pretty extreme." She traced the tats on his neck and chest. "Even for body art, you tip the scale, my dear."

"Yeah, when I look in the mirror, I actually scare *myself*," he quipped.

"Oh, come on, I think you're cute."

"You do?" He frowned. "That makes me wonder about you."

"What?" She reached for a throw pillow and smacked him with it.

Derek laughed and threw up an arm to defend himself. Then he sobered up. "You know when you were going through all those changes . . . I wondered how far you were going to go. Your tattoo was one of the things that scared me. That's why I gave you such a hard time. I was scared you wouldn't be able to draw the line and then you would do something really crazy."

She cocked an eyebrow. "Like come in with my body covered in tattoos?"

"Yeah, something like *that.*"

Derek pulled her into his arms. He kissed her slowly. Then he pulled back until their lips were almost touching. He felt her breath quicken. Kendal stood up, took his hand, and pulled him to her bedroom.

⁂

They lay tangled together in the sheets, releasing all the tension of the day. Afterwards, Derek fell asleep. He dreamed he was back in high school. But this time he felt a sense of power as he pushed hard on the doors to exit the building.

He stood at the top of the stairs with a clear view of his mother and grandmother on the sidewalk. They were smiling and waiting to pick him up. He went running out to hug and kiss them both. With a full heart, he turned to see Kendal waiting at the top of the steps. He waved for her to come down.

Before she could reach him, Derek woke with a pounding pulse. He slid quietly out of bed so as not to wake her. He walked into the bathroom and flipped on the light.

As he had hoped, many of the tattoos were gone from his torso. He still had the teardrop on his face and the markings along his jaw, continuing down his neck. His chest only had the red heart with the rose and vine.

Gathering his courage, Derek turned to look at his back. The faces of the monsters were gone! He still had the angel and the serpent, but the spider and its web had vanished.

Examining his body in the mirror, it dawned on him that what the doctor had said was true. He had let go of his anger with the realization that there wasn't anyone to hate anymore. The constant, low-level anxiety had started to diminish. Adding newfound romantic feelings, he felt the budding of a fresh start in life.

He whispered a prayer of gratitude, turned off the light, and quietly crawled back into bed.

Chapter 21

Kendal came out to the patio with her morning coffee in hand. "I still can't believe so many of them have disappeared! That's fantastic."

Derek felt calmer and more relaxed than he had in years. "I was pretty surprised myself."

She slid into the opposite chair. "You're still cute, I guess."

"You mean you liked me better with the fully illustrated face?"

She frowned and blew on her coffee. "I'm trying to decide."

Derek jumped up from his chair. Kendal screamed and bolted back into the living room. Brutus screeched in imitation, running back and forth along his perch.

Derek held his palms up. "Don't worry Brutus, I won't hurt her."

"You better not lay a finger me," Kendal laughed.

"You don't think so?" Derek lunged. He grabbed her around the waist and they both collapsed onto the sofa.

"Okay, okay," Kendal gasped. "I give up."

"Do you think you've learned your lesson?" He kissed her . . . which led straight back to bed.

An hour later, Kendal curled up next to him, tracing the lines on his chest.

"They do turn me on, you know," she murmured.

"Uh-oh." The corner of his mouth twitched. "Does this mean that if my tattoos all disappear our relationship is over?"

"I don't know." She looked up at him. "You aren't planning on going back to being the stuffy old Dr. Hollinger, are you?"

He chuckled. "I don't think I could ever be that person again. But Kendal . . . these last couple of days have given me a spark of new life. I can feel the lift in my spirit. So I'm going to focus on how to communicate better. I want to be a kinder, more compassionate person who shows empathy and respect—especially to you."

"I like the sound of that," she said with a smile.

"This is the happiest I can ever remember being in my life," he told her seriously. "I don't want that to change." Derek winked. "So if I do lose these tattoos and have to go out and get more to keep you happy, it will be well worth it."

She gave him a reassuring kiss. "Hopefully my affection won't require such drastic measures. Hey, let's go down to the beach and take a walk. Get out of here for a little bit."

"Okay." He threw off the sheet. "But let's take a shower first. You can scrub my back and tell me if any other tattoos are missing."

"Ah, take a shower so I can scrub your back and count tattoos?"

"Sure, why not?" Derek headed for the bathroom.

"Oh, I'm sure I can think of *something* else to keep us entertained," Kendal remarked as she closed the bathroom door behind her.

❧❦❧

They arrived at the beach just before noon. The hot sun was

blazing, and Derek felt glad he had remembered to wear his cap. He looked over at Kendal, who never seemed to forget her fedora. They sat down on a bench to enjoy their ice cream cones.

"I can't remember ever getting ice cream and just sitting and people-watching," Derek remarked.

She took a lick of her rum raisin. "First hot dogs, then ice cream. You can't say I don't know how to show a guy a good time."

Derek laughed. "Quite the opposite."

"You have a lot to catch up on," Kendal said gently. "And I'm just the person to help you."

"Yes, you are," he agreed.

A young mother holding her child's hand walked by. The little girl stopped to stare back at the bench. "Look Mama! Look at the man with all the tattoos!"

The woman blushed and pulled her daughter close. "I am *so* sorry," she said.

"That's okay," they replied in unison, as the woman rushed off.

Derek and Kendal looked at each other and burst into laughter. The shadows lengthened as they sat together, content just to enjoy their ice cream cones and watch the world pass by.

About the Author

Writer, speaker, and certified life coach Monica Broussard is passionate about writing fiction that contains elements of fantasy and keeps the reader intrigued about the lead character's motives. She also writes an occasional article for her hometown's magazine, *SeaCliff Living*. She belongs to Toastmasters International and enjoys attending national writers' conferences.

Born in North Carolina on a Marine Corps base, Monica now lives in "Surf City," Huntington Beach, California, with her husband of thirty-seven years. She has enjoyed various occupations over the years, but her favorite job is the one she's doing now—writing. *Twenty-One Tattoos* is her debut novel.

For more about her writing, visit her website:
MonicaBroussardAuthor.com

www.ingramcontent.com/pod-product-compliance
Lightning Source LLC
Chambersburg PA
CBHW020111310726
48970CB00002B/583